Sins of a Hustla

Lock Down Publications and
Ca$h Presents

Sins of a Hustla

A Novel by ASAD

Lock Down Publications
P.O. Box 870494
Mesquite, Tx 75187

Visit our website
www.lockdownpublications.com

Lock Down Publications
Like our page on Facebook: Lock Down Publications
@
www.facebook.com/lockdownpublications.ldp
Cover design and layout by: **Dynasty Cover Me**
Book interior design by: **Shawn Walker**
Edited by**: Jill Alicea**

Stay Connected with Us!

Text **LOCKDOWN** to 22828 to stay up-to-date with new releases, sneak peaks, contests and more…

Submission Guideline.

Submit the first three chapters of your completed manuscript to ldpsubmissions@gmail.com, subject line: Your book's title. The manuscript must be in a .doc file and sent as an attachment. Document should be in Times New Roman, double spaced and in size 12 font. Also, provide your synopsis and full contact information. If sending multiple submissions, they must each be in a separate email.

Have a story but no way to send it electronically? You can still submit to LDP/Ca$h Presents. Send in the first three chapters, written or typed, of your completed manuscript to:

LDP: Submissions Dept
Po Box 870494
Mesquite, Tx 75187

DO NOT send original manuscript. Must be a duplicate.

Provide your synopsis and a cover letter containing your full contact information.

Thanks for considering LDP and Ca$h Presents.

ASAD

Chapter 1
November 2008

"Max? Max, wake up, you're gonna be late for school."

"*A 'ight*, Mom," I replied in frustration, still not opening my eyes or moving from beneath the warmth of my comforter.

This was the second time she'd come in to wake me up, but we both knew it wasn't because she was terribly concerned about me getting an education. She wanted something from me. I waited until I heard my bedroom door close before I nudged the girl hiding beneath the comforter, signaling that it was okay for her to stick her head back out.

"Max, how the hell am I supposed to sneak out of here?" Lilliana whispered.

It was hard not to openly laugh at the fear filling up her light brown eyes, especially since I knew my mom was the cause of it, but I managed to keep a straight face.

"What you scared of, sweetheart? You know that you've got no worries when you're with me."

"I believe that everywhere *except* in your mom's house," she whispered fiercely.

I thought all you Dominican chicks were badasses," I replied, smiling at her.

My smart remark had her beautiful face screwed up and her eyes shooting daggers at me, which indicated that I was about to be on the receiving end of the Latina fire I'd questioned.

"It's cool, Pinky, she'll be leaving in a few minutes," I said, kissing her soft lips gently.

"I hate it when you call me that."

"But you love when I'm face down in your pinkness, right?" I asked seductively while walking my fingers down her naked flesh.

Within seconds, her light chocolate complexion became infused with a red hue, indicating her blushing and her arousal.

"S-stop playing, boy, I'm not doing *shit* while your mom is up and roaming around," she insisted.

Part of me wanted to push the issue simply because I knew that I was Lilliana's weakness, but I knew my mother well enough to know that she'd keep coming back until she got what she wanted.

"Stay right here," I demanded, kissing her quickly before sliding out of bed and pulling on a pair of Carolina blue basketball shorts. The way her eyes locked in on my 6'3", 240 pound frame damn near made me blush, but I'd learned two years ago as a freshman in high school how to transform my body into a work of art worthy of stares.

"Hurry back," she said, licking her lips slowly.

Without bothering to count, I grabbed some money off my dresser on my way out of my bedroom in search of my mom. Not surprisingly, I found her pacing the floor in her bedroom.

"How much do you need?" I asked.

"Huh?"

"Come on, Mom, let's not play games this morning. How much do you need?" I asked again, fighting not to show my frustration.

"I, uh, well, we need a few groceries and - "

"Mom, *I'll* take care of the groceries and any bills that need immediate attention. Just tell me how much you need for *you.*"

The shame I saw in her dark brown eyes made me feel bad because I knew it was hard for her having to depend on her sixteen-year-old son for everything - including her drug habits. I knew the shame wouldn't stop her from taking money from me to feed her demons though, just like my disgust for her drug use wouldn't stop me from giving her money. Most of the world saw her as a skinny, toothless junkie who looked like life had steamrolled her, but to me, she was my mother. She would always be my beautiful black queen no matter what she did, and I would rather her get money from me than be in the streets turning tricks. Nah, not my momma.

"I, uh, should be good with twenty dollars," she replied softly.

"Make sure you eat something," I said, giving her a fifty dollar bill.

I kissed her quickly on the cheek before making my way back to my room. I thought Lilliana might have made a run for it while I had my mom distracted, but as soon as I closed my bedroom door, she popped back up from beneath the covers.

"We good?" she asked.

"Yeah."

She immediately tossed the covers aside, revealing her gorgeous naked body to me accompanied by a smile of devilish intentions.

"So we're not going to school?" I asked, tossing my money back on my dresser and moving back towards the bed.

"It's my senior year and I'm only two credits short, so I don't have to be there when the first bell rings. If you're worried about being a little late…"

She let the rest of her sentence trail off as she slowly spread her legs, revealing her pussy to me like a beautiful rose. I could feel my mouth watering because we both knew that it was this part of the rose that made it possible to deal with her thorns. I dropped my shorts, stepped out of them, and picked up a condom from my supply on the nightstand by my bed. I took pleasure in the anticipation I saw in her eyes as she watched me roll the latex down my long, hard dick before climbing onto the bed. She welcomed me with open legs and arms, allowing me to dive deep inside her sweetest secret while catching her sigh of contentment as it rolled off her tongue. Within the first few moments, she knew that this wasn't no slow jam because I was delivering dick hard like rock music, trying to play pinball with her organs. I made sure to keep my mouth on hers, knowing that it was the only way to keep her screams muffled, but eventually, not even that was enough. After quickly covering her face with a pillow I leaned back far enough to put her legs on my shoulders. And then I dove deeper, testing the strength of her pussy walls with each blow. It only took ten minutes of my thug love to have her squirting all over me and have her body shaking like she was having a seizure. I kept pounding her for five more minutes though until I couldn't fight off my own climax, and then I collapsed beside her.

"Why you-why you do that?" she panted breathlessly.

"Because y-you wanted it."

"Yeah b-but you almost suffocated m-me," she replied, elbowing me in the chest.

Her tone suggested that she was upset, but the look on her face was pure sexual satisfaction.

"Sorry babe," I said, pulling her towards me and holding her close. We stayed like that until our heartbeats returned to normal and the sweat on our skin started to cool.

"You think your mom is still here?" she asked.

"No, I heard her leave while you were under the pillow."

"So why did you keep the damn thing on my face?" she asked hostilely, elbowing me again when I began to laugh.

"Babe, I was caught up in the moment. You know that pussy is hypnotizing."

"Whatever. Don't do that again or I'm gonna kick your ass," she threatened, grabbing ahold of my dick and squeezing it hard.

"You know what you're gonna have to do if you wake this thing up, so you better stop playing."

She held on for a few moments longer, her eyes alight with the defiance to challenge me, but eventually, she let me go.

"Are you going to school or not?" she asked, climbing out of bed and searching for her clothes.

"Probably. What about you?"

"I gotta go home first, but yeah, I'll be there," she replied, shimmying into her pink lace panties.

"Go home first? Babe, it's already seven a.m. Why are you going all the way to the other side of the city? And don't say it's because you need clothes because you've got *plenty* in my closet."

"It's not that, but you know my dad is gonna trip about me not coming home all night."

"Even though you're eighteen years old, *and* he thinks that you spent the night at one of your girlfriend's houses on some late night studying shit?" I asked with a raised eyebrow.

"Stop acting like you don't know my dad. And it don't matter how old I am, I'll always be his little princess."

"If he only knew what a *dirty* little princess you were," I replied, laughing.

I was just barely able to duck the shoe she threw at me, but that didn't stop my laughter as I got out of bed to get myself together. Lilliana was a good girl from a good family, and there weren't too many of either of those things in Fayetteville, NC, so I could understand her dad's over-protectiveness. I loved Lilliana though, and I'd told her pops that to his face because I thought that would make him cool with our relationship. But he was still frosty, which forced her to lie about her whereabouts. I wasn't out to cause a problem between her and her dad or anyone in her family, so far the most part, I kept my mouth shut. It did bother me a little though because I knew I was a good dude, and I treated my girl right.

"Ugh, you ain't gonna take a shower?" she asked, wrinkling her nose up at me.

"Oh, so you got a problem with me smelling like you all of a sudden?" I retorted.

"I better be the *only* woman you smell like, but marinating in my pussy juices all day could have you living a little foul, babe."

"Don't worry, I'll take a shower before I make it to class," I replied, going to my closet and grabbing a black hoodie and some matching jeans.

"Before you make it to class? Why do I suddenly feel like you're not going straight to school?"

"I gotta make a quick stop, but it ain't nothing serious," I replied vaguely.

My statement made her put her hands on her thick hips as she rose to her full 5'2" height while giving me a look that said, "Nigga, I ain't stupid."

Of course I already knew that she wasn't stupid because she made straight A's effortlessly, but she knew that I had to do what was necessary to make ends meet. That didn't necessarily mean that she *agreed* with me getting to the money though.

"Stop looking at me like that. I gotta handle something real quick, but it ain't *nothing* serious," I insisted.

"Who are you handling it with?"

Her asking me that question put a look on my face that she was all too familiar with because I carried myself like Don Corleone, and I didn't allow her to ask me about my business.

"I don't understand how you think it's fair that you get to run the streets doing whatever the fuck you want, but you expect me to be at home in the dark," she said, continuing to get dressed in frustration.

"Babe, we've had this conversation so you already know what it is. The way I live my life ain't for you, and it don't need to rub off on you. You're *almost* free of the bullshit and poverty of Fayetteville, so will you please just focus on graduation and going to college?"

"Sure I will, if you'll do the same thing."

"Lilliana, the bills don't pay themselves," I replied patiently.

"I get that, but maybe if your mom would - "

"Don't!" I growled immediately, stopping her from saying some shit that would cause more than an argument.

"I forgot, you don't like to hear the truth. I'll see you at school," she said, gathering the rest of her stuff and storming out of my room.

A few seconds later I heard the front door slam, but I shook that shit off and got dressed. After sending a text to my partner in today's particular crime, I grabbed everything I needed, including my Taurus Millennium G2 9mm pistol, and headed out to my car. The streets talked, so I did my best to keep a low profile, but my old school navy blue box Chevy on twenty-fours was my baby. When I'd first started getting to the money a couple years back I'd done the typical shit and splurged on a car, but not a car that would stick out in the hood. The new age dope boys wanted to ride around in something foreign, but I wasn't a dope boy, and I wasn't stupid. My box Chevy had rims, a knocking sound system, tint, and a couple televisions, but that wasn't any different from dudes who worked a regular nine to five job. Hiding in plain sight was the key to longevity, and I reminded myself of that no matter how much money I made.

I slid behind the wheel of my ride and made the quick fifteen minute drive to Sophia's house, making sure to keep my eyes open for anything that made me feel some type of way. I'd learned early on that your instincts were the *only* thing you could trust in the streets, and I listened to mine religiously. I felt like today would be a good day as I knocked on Sophia's apartment door.

I didn't expect her to answer wearing nothing, clutching her pistol.

Chapter 2

"You expecting somebody other than me?" I asked, raising my hands in the air to show that I was coming in peace.

"No, but I thought that I heard something while I was in the shower, before you knocked. Come in," she said, turning around and walking back into the apartment.

I'd known Sophia since elementary school and she was one of the few people that I considered a real friend. This wasn't the first time I'd seen her naked though, and I had to admit that over the years the view had only gotten better.

"I see you've been working out," I said, closing the door behind us as I followed her down the hallway.

"You can stop looking at my ass anytime now," she replied over her shoulder.

"Shit, I'm a man and I'm not ashamed to look. Besides, you're 5'1" and like 119 pounds, and you're *all ass*, so what else am I supposed to look at?"

"First of all, the fact that you *still* remember some of my measurements is crazy because you ain't had to carry me on your back through the high school hallways since I dropped out last year. And secondly, I've *always* been all ass because I'm black and Mexicana. This booty ain't going *nowhere*," she replied, slapping her left ass cheek for emphasis.

For a second I got lost in the way her backside was jiggling, but she pulled a pair of cotton panties on to bring me back to reality.

"You shouldn't be looking at me anyway. You got a girl, remember?"

"It don't matter where I get my appetite as long as I go home to eat," I replied, smiling.

"So you wouldn't eat me if I wanted you to?" she asked seductively, walking right up to me and forcing me to back into a wall.

"I, uh, I mean, um - "

Her instant laughter made me swallow whatever lame shit I was about to say, but I wasn't embarrassed because Sophia had always had a weird effect on me. She was the only girl my age who could do it too, but deep down, she was too much of a softy when it came to me to take advantage of the situation.

"You're *so* funny," I said sarcastically.

"Yeah, I know. It's a good thing I wasn't serious though because you smell like another female, and I don't do sloppy seconds."

I opened my mouth to say something, but she was already back to getting dressed. Despite being only sixteen, Sophia lived in a studio apartment by herself because she'd gotten emancipated by the courts. I couldn't blame her because life on her own was way better than the abuse and violence she'd grown up with. Shit like that changed a person. But Sophia was caring - well, at least when it came to people she fucked with. She was also brutally honest and spoke her mind about *everything*, which was why her comment about me smelling like Lilliana didn't surprise me.

"Don't sit on my bed," she said, forcing me to pause in mid-squat.

"Damn, it's like that?"

"Yeah, nigga, I didn't want you and your bitch's scent on my sheets. Is that too much to ask?"

"Maybe if you had yours and somebody *else's* scent on your sheets, you wouldn't be in suck a cranky mood," I replied, smiling when she blew me a kiss with her middle finger. "One day we'll fuck, but for today, let's get down to the business. What's the play?" I asked, getting serious.

16

"Dope house on the north side. Nothing-ass niggas actually got kids living out of the same spot they trappin' out of, and they keep the stash there too."

"How many dudes?" I asked.

"Two or three, same amount of females, but everybody gets high on their own supply."

"Who's their connect?"

"Don't know and don't care," she replied dispassionately, tucking her gun into the back of her hip-hugging blue jeans before pulling on a black wife beater.

"No bra," I commented, smiling.

"Not necessary when you got firm titties. Stay focused."

"A'ight, so how do you know about the spot we 'bout to hit?" I asked.

"I know one of the nigga's baby mamas, and let's just say that my tongue works better than his. Plus she wants out, but of course doesn't have the money to start over, so I promised her I'd help her."

"And you think her dude is just gonna let that happen? I mean, we ain't the police so it won't be like this nigga is locked up once the heist is over," I said.

"Let me worry about all that. We need to get on the move because the perfect time to run in is while the kids are going out to school. Lydia said it's usually only one dude awake serving fiends this early, but I'll text her to make sure once we get there."

"You got the ride already?" I asked.

"Yeah, it's out front. Come on," she said, slipping her Nike boots on while grabbing a backpack off the floor and leading the way out of her apartment.

I followed her outside and to the back of the parking lot, where we got into a black Dodge Caravan.

"Nice wheels," I commented sarcastically.

"As long as it blends in and appears non-threatening, I'm good with it," she replied, grabbing the key from above the visor and starting the engine. Before pulling off she passed me the backpack, and I opened it to inspect its contents. I'd expected to find masks of some sort and maybe some extra ammo, but I found more than that.

"Okay, um, why are there ball gags, zip ties, and needles in here?" I asked, looking at here with the side eye.

"We've gotta be prepared for anything, and it's only two of us, so we need to restrain mu'fuckas in order to work faster."

"Do you know where everything is at?" I asked, pulling a Mac-11 from the bag and checking the clip.

"Yeah, Lydia gave me the layout. We should be in and out in under ten minutes."

"We've only got a half an hour to get there, because school will be in session," I said.

"I got this," she replied, speeding out of the apartment complex.

I let her focus on navigating us to our destination while I got everything ready for the move we were about to put down. I knew that if Lilliana could see me now she'd lose her *entire* mind, and that was part of the reason I'd downplayed what my mission was for the day. It wasn't as if I took risks like this every day, but I believed in getting money with versatility. Last week I'd turned a nice profit from a shipment of cell phones that had fallen off the back of a truck. Bottom line was that if it was about money, then I was about it - except for selling dope. That was the one thing that I *couldn't* and *wouldn't* do, not for any reason or any amount of money. I knew that Lilliana would probably prefer that I be a full-time drug dealer instead of risking my life in a more insane way, but I'd rather lose my life than lose my soul. By the time I'd gloved up, wiped our guns down, and loaded the extra clips, Sophia was bringing the van to a stop on a street lined with low income single family homes.

"It's the third house on the left, the white one with the dingy blue shutters," Sophia said, pulling out her phone and sending a text.

"Bars on the windows. Is the door reinforced?"

"Yeah, that's why we're going in when she comes out with the kids. There's three of them in elementary school," she replied.

"Is that why you chose clown masks?"

"No, I chose clown masks because I like clowns. Especially evil clowns," she replied, smiling at me.

"*That's* not weird."

Before she could respond her phone went off, capturing her undivided attention.

"Show time," she said.

I quickly passed her a clown mask and her Mac-11 before slipping my own mask on. She eased the van forward slowly until we were one house down, and then masked up before putting the backpack on her back.

"One nigga is in the kitchen bagging up, there's a couple junkies in the living room, and there's two niggas asleep in the back bedroom with the other bitches. We don't worry about the smokers. The first thing we gotta do is get to the kitchen and shut him up before he can make any noise. After that we take the mu'fuckas in the bedroom, and then we get to work. Any questions?" she asked.

"What does your pussy taste like?"

Even though she was shaking her head I still heard her laughter through the mask she was wearing. It had become a habit of mine to say some off the wall shit to lighten the mood before we got down to business, almost like wearing a pair of lucky socks.

"Here we go," Sophia said, directing my attention to the front door that was now open.

Three little kids appeared in the doorway, along with a light-skinned young chick. It was obvious as they walked out of the house that the children's minds were already preoccupied with the school day ahead, but the woman that I assumed was Lydia was scanning the street.

"Can she be any more obvious?" I asked, looking around to see if anyone was watching her.

"Don't worry about her. Just stay focused, because she didn't close the door all the way."

We waited until Lydia and the kids were headed up the sidewalk away from the house before creeping out of the van and making a beeline across the sparse grass towards our target.

"Straight to the kitchen," Sophia whispered, before leading the way into the house like we lived there. I followed her lead, barely scanning the living room we passed, but keeping my eyes open for any threats.

"You breathe heavy and you die," Sophia whispered, running down on the short, stocky nigga sitting at the kitchen table.

I could tell by the instant tension in his body that he desperately wanted to reach for the black 9mm Beretta that was on the table in front of him, but he was smart enough to know that he'd never get it in time. Sophia moved swiftly behind him and smacked him mercilessly over the head with her gun. Somehow she managed not to let him hit the floor or take a nose dive in the pile of coke on the table, but instead, she pulled his unconscious body to the floor quietly.

"Cover me," she demanded, putting her gun down and pulling her backpack off.

I turned around, aiming my gun back up the short hallway we'd just come down with my finger on the trigger. I didn't want to shoot anybody, but if the choice was them or me, there was no question which way I was gonna vote. Within thirty seconds Sophia was back at my side, and I looked back to find our first victim with a ball gag in his mouth and zip ties holding him like a lost lover returned.

"Back bedroom," Sophia whispered, leading the way down a side hallway that we'd passed.

Once we got to the door she stopped and put her ear to it, trying to listen for any movement on the other side. After a few seconds she gave a decisive nod before slowly turning the doorknob carefully. We crept into the room, where we found two couples fast asleep on separate air mattresses. Using hand gestures, Sophia told me to collect the guns laying around the room while she went into her backpack again and started pulling shit out. I collected all the weapons I saw, stashing them in the now empty backpack, and waited for her to signal that it was time to wake everybody up. When she gave me the nod I moved to one of the air mattresses, bent down, and tapped the nigga sleeping on the lip with the short barrel of the Mac-11 in my grip.

"No sudden moves or you lose your head, literally," I whispered.

The dark brown eyes staring back at me were mirrors of confusion, which transformed to anger, until fear finally bullied its way in. With fear came the understanding that any dumb shit would most definitely result in a loss of life.

"Arm out," Sophia demanded, kneeling beside the man with a full syringe in her hand.

I wanted to ask her what she was filling these mu'fuckas up with, but honestly I didn't care. In my opinion it was poetic justice to have them high out of their mind. She jabbed him in the arm not so gently, and within seconds, he was back in the land of heavy slumber. After binding and gagging him, we quickly repeated the process until everyone in the room was unconscious whether they wanted to be or not.

"Where's the stash?" I asked.

"Behind the refrigerator. Come on."

We made our way back to the kitchen and pushed the fridge away from the wall to find a huge hole in the wall.

"They've got a *serious* rodent problem," I said.

"We need to hurry. We're right on top of the ten minute mark. Start stuffing the backpack while I look for another bag," she replied, tossing me her bag before disappearing.

I started with the drugs, grabbing the two kilos of coke and the compressed two pounds of weed, lining the bottom of the backpack over top of the pistols. That didn't leave a lot of room for the money, but I stuffed stack after stack inside until I could barely zip the backpack closed. I'd just swung it onto my back when Sophia reappeared with another backpack, and she immediately started filling it.

"Let's go," she said once we'd emptied out the hole in the wall.

I led the way back towards the front of the house, becoming more excited with each step I took because we were seconds away from pulling off our biggest heist yet.

"Hey, you got anymore - "

My gun going off silenced the request the junkie was about to make. Truthfully I hadn't meant to shoot her, but she'd popped out of the living room and startled me. It wasn't until I went to move past her slumping figure that I'd realized what I'd done.

"What the fuck are you stopping for? Leave that bitch! Somebody *definitely* heard them shots, which means we gotta *go!*" Sophia said, trying to push me towards the door.

"I-I can't leave her."

"What? Nigga, have you lost your fucking mind! That junkie bitch ain't worth your freedom *or* mine so - "

"She's not some junkie bitch, Sophia! She's my mother."

ASAD

Chapter 3

"Mom? Mom, can you hear me? Come on, you gotta stay awake," I said, fighting against the panic that was trying to paralyze me while rocking her back and forth in my arms.

"M-max, I'm s-sorry," she whispered, grimacing in pain.

"Shhh, you don't need to apologize, just stay awake and keep pressure on your stomach. Sophia, drive *faster*."

"Bruh, we've got guns and dope on us."

"I don't give a fuck about *none* of that, get us to the goddamn hospital!" I yelled, giving into the fear I felt pumping through my veins.

Luckily, only one bullet of the three round burst I'd fired had hit my mom, but I'd seen enough TV to know how bad a gut shot could be. I could look into her eyes and tell that she was too high to feel the full force of pain that came with a wound like she had, but that wouldn't stop her from bleeding out. I couldn't be the cause of my own mother's death, and I *damn* sure couldn't watch her die in my arms. Thankfully I didn't have to shout this at Sophia because I felt the van leap when she pushed the gas pedal to the floor. Part of me wanted to yell at my mom for being in that particular dope house, but the guilt I felt about not only giving her the money to score, but also shooting her, was choking me. This entire situation was all my fault.

"M-max."

"Mom, don't try to talk. We're getting you to the hospital," I said emotionally.

"I love you, Max," she whispered, giving me one of her rare smiles that could still light up her face despite the years of mistreatment that were visible.

"I love you too. Just hold on a little bit longer, we're almost there," I promised, swiping at the tears that were falling from my eyes onto her.

For a split second she got a blank look on her face that stopped my heart, but just as quickly, her eyes refocused on me and she nodded that she heard me.

"Sophia," I said, distressed.

"We're here," Sophia replied, bringing the stolen minivan to a screeching halt before she hopped out and opened the sliding side door.

"Get out of here. I'll call you," I said, holding my mom tighter and climbing out of the van.

"But Max - "

"Sophia, go! There will be *way* too many questions to answer. You gotta go," I insisted.

Despite the reluctance I saw in her hazel eyes, I knew she understood the truth that I was speaking, but it was hard for her because she was loyal to a fault.

"I'll call you," I promised.

She kissed me quickly on the lips before hopping back in the driver's seat.

"Help, I need help!" I yelled, rushing towards the emergency room entrance.

Within seconds of coming through the automatic doors I was surrounded by nurses and my mom was being whisked away on a stretcher.

"Max!" she called out.

"It's okay, Mom, I'll be right here," I promised, still struggling to gather my emotions.

I was beyond hurt over the dramatic turn my life had taken in the past ten minutes, but I knew it would take a clear head to deal with the nurses. And the cops.

"Sir, do you know the victim?" a petite white woman in green scrubs asked.

"She's my mom."

"Okay, well I need you to come with me to fill out some paperwork. That's all you can do for her at this moment, but I promise you that she's in the best hands and receiving the absolute best care available," the nurse assured me.

I wanted desperately to follow my mother into the operating room, but I knew that wouldn't be allowed, so I followed the nurse to her station. Answering tedious questions for an hour allowed me to go emotionally numb so that by the time the detective arrived, I was in the right frame of mind to deal with him.

"Mr. Cooper? My name is Detective Brewer."

I looked up from my seat next to the nurse's desk to find a beefy black hand extended my way, but I didn't shake it. Instead I sized up the six foot, 250 pound, thick-necked black guy in the gray suit that fit like a second skin - but not in the expensive, tailored way. His eyes were a dull brown, not to be confused with someone possessing a low IQ though, and I knew that because of how closely he was observing me right now.

"I've got blood on my hands," I said, forcing him to retract his paw.

"I'm here about what happened to your mom. Can you tell me what happened?"

"I don't know what happened. All I know is someone shot my mom," I replied, looking down at the dried blood caked beneath my fingernails.

"*Who* shot her?" Brewer asked.

His tone was slightly accusatory, but not in a way that suggested he knew what had actually happened, more so like he believed I knew who'd done it.

27

"If I knew who shot my mom, you'd be going to scrape his body off the motherfuckin' pavement," I replied aggressively.

"Where was she shot?" Brewer asked, unflinching in the face of my growing anger.

"I don't know where she was shot. I found her on my way to school."

"Where *exactly* did you find her?" Brewer persisted.

"In our apartment building."

"Did you hear a struggle or any gunshots before that?" Brewer asked.

"No, but even if I had, it wouldn't have been anything out of the ordinary in the projects," I replied truthfully.

"Do you know of anyone who would want to hurt your mother?" Brewer asked.

"Look, let's not act like my mom's life choices ain't obvious because I know you've seen her arrest records for drug possession. She's a junkie, and that brings her into contact with the type of motherfuckers who shoot first and never bother with questions. That pretty much makes the list of suspects endless, but don't worry, I'll deal with the person responsible," I vowed.

"Mr. Cooper, I advise you to let me do my job and not make any foolish attempts at taking justice into your own hands. That won't help your mom or her situation."

"You're talking to me like I'm some kid that still believes in the illusion of the police into protect and serve, *Detective*. I know the cops ain't shit and they don't care about what happens in the projects, so real justice won't come from you or your kind," I replied with brutal honesty.

I saw anger flash quickly in his eyes, but he tucked it away and slipped back into his professional persona.

"My kind, huh? Well, I would love to educate you on my *kind*, but that statement you made speaks volumes about your ignorance of how the world really works. I'll give you some free advice though. Let the cops handle this, or you might find yourself laying in the bed next to your mother, *if* you're lucky enough to survive being shot. You never know, maybe it was *your kind* who was responsible for what happened to your mom. After all, you young punks are all alike."

With that statement, Detective Brewer turned and walked away, leaving me fuming with anger and drowning in guilt. I was sure that he didn't know how close his words hit home, and that he only said what he did because of the generalized statement I'd made about the cops not being shit. I'd just been speaking the truth, most cops weren't shit, but neither was a nigga who shot his own momma.

"Mr. Cooper, your mom is out of surgery and will be moved to the ICU shortly. You'll be allowed to see her briefly, but only if you promise not to cause a problem when you're asked to leave," the petite nurse in the green scrubs stated.

"What's your name?" I asked.

"Megan."

"Okay, Megan, I'm sure that's the routine speech you give all family members to prevent hysterical behavior, but this is my *mother* we're talking about. I don't want to leave her side," I said.

"I understand that, but no one outside of medical staff and personnel is allowed in the ICU around the clock. Once your mom is moved into her own room I'll personally set you up a cot by her bed, okay?"

I could see the compassion in her blue/grey eyes, but I still wanted to argue and act a fool. Luckily for Megan my common sense won out over my warring emotions, and I nodded my acceptance reluctantly.

"Okay, if you'll follow me I'll - "

"Oh my God, babe, what the fuck *happened*?" Lilliana asked, rushing around the nurse's desk towards me.

"What are you doing here?" I asked, surprised to see her, but more than grateful.

"Sophia hit me up and told me to get down here because your mom was in the hospital. Whose blood are you covered in?"

I couldn't bring myself to utter the devastating words of truth so I simply took her hand in my own. "Come on," I said, nodding towards Megan to lead the way.

I could feel Lilliana's fingers begin to tremble as we followed closely behind the nurse, but she didn't let go of my hand, and I drew strength from her act of comfort. My knees wobbled a little when we passed under the sign that said we were entering the intensive care unit, but I didn't break stride because I knew I had to face what I'd done.

"You've got ten minutes," Megan said, stopping and stepping aside when we reached my mom's temporary room.

"Wait a minute, what the fuck?"

"It's okay, babe. Thank you Megan," I said, stopping Lilliana's tirade before she got us kicked out early.

"How she only gonna give you ten minutes?" Lilliana asked once Megan had walked away.

"I won't be able to stay with her while she's in intensive care, and arguing with the nurse won't change that," I replied softly, staring intently at my mother.

In my wildest dreams I never could've imagined that the women who'd given me life could be laid up in a hospital bed fighting for *her* life because of some shit I'd done. The pain I felt in this moment required words that hadn't been invented yet to describe it. It was only matched by my guilt.

"Wait right here," I said, letting her hand go and walking slowly to stand by my mother's side.

She looked fragile, yet more peaceful than I'd seen her in years.

"I'm sorry, Mom, I never meant for this to happen," I whispered, taking her hand in both of mine.

To feel her warmth brought my tears back, and I didn't bother trying to fight them. I understood that being in the ICU meant shit was still touch and go, but my mom was *alive*, and I was thankful for that.

"You're a fighter, Wanda Cooper, you've been one your entire life, and I need you to fight harder than ever now. I *need you*, Mom. I know I act like I don't, but I promise you that you're still my world and I need you. Fight, Mom. Please," I said, leaning down and kissing both of her cheeks and her forehead.

Even though I didn't wanna leave, I knew I couldn't stay or I'd break down completely. With a heavy heart I gently laid my mom's hand on the bed and retreated quietly from the room. Without a word, Lilliana reclaimed my hand and we made our way out of the hospital into the mid-morning sunlight. I climbed in the passenger side of her white Honda Accord, leaned my seat all the way back, and closed my eyes. As badly as I wanted to, I wasn't able to escape the nightmare I was living in because the morning's events were playing on the back of my eyelids in HD. With each passing moment I hated myself more and more, and I had no idea what to do with those feelings.

"Where do you wanna go?" Lilliana asked after we'd been riding in silence for a while.

Part of me wanted to go home so I could simply shut the world out, but I knew everything in that apartment would remind me of my mom.

"Take me to Sophia's," I replied.

"Sophia's? Why? Are you gonna tell me what happened?"

"My mom got shot," I said simply.

"Shot? Who would want to kill your mom?"

I knew I could trust Lilliana with the truth, but emotionally I was too drained to deal with the questions that would surely follow.

"I don't know, babe, I don't know what happened. I don't wanna talk about it," I replied.

We rode on without saying anything else until she brought the car to a stop in front of Sophia's apartment building.

"Why are we here, Max?"

"I gotta tie up some loose ends with Sophia real quick and - "

"Now? You think it's a good idea to handle business *now*?" she asked, clearly shocked and frustrated.

"Lilliana, I don't have the energy to fight with you right now, so let me take care of this and we'll meet up later."

"I'm not trying to fight with you, I'm just trying to understand what the hell you're thinking. I mean, your mom is in the hospital and you're worried about some business bullshit," she replied, becoming more annoyed.

"There's nothing I can do for my mom right now, and sitting around thinking about what happened will drive me crazy because I can't control shit about what happens next. So I'm gonna focus on some shit I *can* control."

"Max I know you're hurting, but - "

"Lilliana, just *stop!*" I said angrily.

I knew she had good intentions in her heart, but she couldn't begin to understand what I was going through or how I was feeling. If she kept trying to convince me otherwise, she'd simply become an easy target for my anger, and she didn't deserve that.

"I'll call you later," I said, opening the door and stepping out.

I hadn't meant to hurt her feelings, but when I glanced back, I could tell by the look on her face I'd done just that.

Despite my love for her, I still walked away and into Sophia's building because I knew I couldn't give her feelings the attention she needed and deserved.

Sophia answered her door after my first round of knocks, immediately stepping to the side and allowing me to come in. It felt like an eternity had passed since I was in this same space cracking jokes while we discussed out latest plans for a quick come up. Everything had definitely changed in the blink of an eye, and right now, I'd give anything to go back in time.

"How is she?" Sophia asked.

"She made it through surgery, but she's still in the ICU."

"Cops come?" she asked, closing and locking the door behind us.

"Yeah, but it was routine questions. Why'd you call Lilliana?" I asked, looking at her.

"I figured you'd need the support, even though I felt some type of way about you forcing me to leave."

"I did need the support, and you *know* why I made you leave. Let's finish up the business," I said, taking a seat on her bed.

"That's not why you're here, Max, and we can deal with that later."

"That *is* why I came back, and - "

"No, you came back because you're going crazy inside, and you can't explain why to anybody, not even Lilliana. I've known you a long time and we've been through a lot together, but this is different. I can look in your eyes and see how lost you are, but you're not gonna go through this alone. I promise," she said sincerely.

I could feel my heart hammering in my chest as relief washed over me like a summer rain, and I was allowed to let the walls down that I'd been hiding behind for the last couple hours. I closed my eyes against my tears, but they still ran wild like a dam full of holes. Because Sophia had been there, I could voice my anguish over what I'd done, but when I opened my eyes and looked at her, I saw that she understood my need for more than verbal expression. She crossed the room, stood in front of me, and pulled me to my feet. I didn't resist when she began to undress me, and within seconds, she had me as completely naked as she was. The look in her eyes told me I didn't have to talk. So I didn't.

Chapter 4

Giving Sophia complete control allowed me to clear my mind of everything except the lust that was quickly clouding my brain, and I welcomed the freedom. She pushed me down onto her bed and climbed on top of me, forcing me flat on my back. Her soft lips found my own at the same time that she grabbed ahold of my dick and guided it inside her feverish wetness. Despite imagining this exact moment a time or two, nothing could've prepared me for how tight her pussy was, or how well we fit together. She kissed me with the same slow thoroughness that she used to ride me, effortlessly adding to the sexual tension that had existed between us for years. Her mouth tasted like good weed and holiday candy canes, and I enjoyed exploring her with my tongue.

"So-ph-ia," I moaned when she began to swivel her hips in little circles while squeezing me tighter from the inside out. She moved my hands to her hips, allowing me to guide her movements any way that I wanted, but when I still didn't take charge, she moved them lower to her juicy ass cheeks.

"You should hold on tight," she whispered seductively against my lips.

Immediately her speed increased, forcing me to heed her warning as the ride got rough in the best possible way. I was thankful that when I closed my eyes, I no longer saw my living nightmare, but instead, the beautiful colors signaling the shock to my senses created by what we were doing. The tighter I grabbed her soft ass, the faster and harder she rode me. When she suddenly sat straight up on the dick I felt her body come alive, and watching her beauty transform had me completely hypnotized. The sway of her succulent titties drew my hands to them, and when I gently squeezed her nipples, I felt her pussy spasm violently.

"I l-like that," she panted without breaking stride.

I tweaked the sensitive gum drops between my fingers again, only harder this time, and the spasms bucked through her until she came with the suddenness of an afternoon tornado. I thought I could hold out and weather her storm, but the non-stop gushing of her pussy had me holding her in place by her hips while my own climax roared to life. Even after we'd stopped throbbing in unison she sat on top of me, looking down into my eyes with a vulnerability that I'd never seen in her.

"You okay?" I asked softly.

"Honestly, I don't know. This changes shit between us," she replied, attempting to move off of me.

I held her in place, forcing her to keep steady eye contact with me.

"Shit between us changed before this, and I know that *you* know that. You were right about why I came back. I didn't anticipate *this* happening, but I needed you, because at this point you're the only person I can turn to, and deep down I knew you'd understand that," I said.

"I do understand. I feel responsible for what happens too because the entire heist was my plan."

"You didn't pull the trigger, so - "

"That don't matter, Max, I'm in this with you. We share the riches and the blame in everything that we do together, no matter how ugly shit gets. I'm *always* with you," she declared sincerely.

We didn't use words like "love" when describing our friendship, but I could see that emotion clearly in her eyes, and I was sure mine mirrored the same message. I pulled her towards me and wrapped my arms around her when she laid her head on my chest. The moment that we were sharing was genuine and unforced, and it felt right. My emotions were still at war with each other inside me, but being with Sophia soothed me in a way that I needed more than I'd ever needed anything in my life. Neither of us had any idea what would happen next, but we had now, and that's all we could hold onto. I laid there looking at the ceiling, inhaling the scent of kiwi melon coming from Sophia's hair until her breathing became deep and even. When my eyes got heavy I followed her lead into the dreamless land of emotional exhaustion. By the time I regained consciousness it was getting dark outside, and surprisingly, Sophia was still in the exact same spot, sleeping on my chest. I didn't want to move or disturb her, but I knew life outside of the cocoon we'd built for ourselves was still moving, and we had to move with it.

"Sophia," I said softly, running my hands up and down her back in a sensual way.

"Hmm?"

"Wake up. We've slept the day away," I replied, kissing the top of her head.

"I was just getting to the good part of my dream," she mumbled, turning her face into my chest and kissing me softly.

"The good part?"

"Mmm hmm. I was right here and we were…"

Her sentences trailed off as she reached down in between our bodies and slid my dick back inside her.

"That is th-the good part," I stammered, holding onto her tighter.

Thirty minutes and two orgasms later, we finally made it out of bed and into the shower. I kept wondering when shit would get awkward between us, but everything flowed naturally like we'd been a couple for years. We even washed each other's backs. Once the shower was over and we had our clothes back on, we both knew it was time for some real talk.

"You can find something to eat in the fridge if you're hungry while I grab the loot," she said, going to the safe she kept in the corner.

I took her up on her offer and made us each a bologna sandwich while she spilt up what we'd taken from the dope house. A big part of me wanted nothing to do with the shit we'd taken because in the end, it had cost me too much. At the same time, I knew that I had to get my mom out of Fayetteville for good because next time it could be someone other than me pulling a jack move, and they wouldn't spare her life.

"A'ight, we got forty-seven thousand in cash, eight guns, two keys of coke, and two pounds of weed. I figured that I'd keep the coke, a pound of weed, and half the guns. You good with that?" she asked.

"You sure you wanna move all that coke?"

"I knew how you feel about selling drugs. The only reason I'm leaving you with a pound of bud is because you're gonna need to smoke in order to stay out of your own head. Nothing you do will be able to change what happened, but being faded will help with the emotional fallout," she replied.

The fact that she was already looking for more ways to help me even when we weren't together reinforced my feelings about it being a good decision to come to her. I loved Lilliana, but I felt no guilt for leaning on Sophia because without her understanding, I'd lose my mind.

"You know that I appreciate you, right?" I asked, handing her the sandwich I'd made.

"Yeah, yeah, you're just mushy because I finally put this good pussy on you."

Her comment made us both laugh, but I could see in her eyes that she understood and felt all that I couldn't say.

"Seriously though, you don't need none of the cash to hold you over? You can always get me straight once you move the coke," I said.

"Don't worry, I've already got a buyer for one key and I'll break the other one down so I can make more money off of it. I'm good."

"A'ight then," I replied before biting my sandwich.

She continued working while she ate, putting everything into the two separate backpacks and pushing one across the table to me.

"What about old girl, Lydia? Don't you need to hit her with some quick cash so that she can disappear before her nigga realizes that it was an inside job?" I asked.

"She ain't gotta worry about her nigga, and I got her taken care of, so don't worry. You just focus on doing what you gotta do to help your mom."

"Why do I feel like there's something you're not telling me?" I asked, looking at her closely.

Her response was a blank stare aimed at me while she chewed her sandwich slowly. My ringing phone stopped me from pressing the issue and had me searching my pockets frantically. When I saw that it was Lilliana calling and that I had five missed calls, I braced myself for another argument.

"Hello?"

"Why the fuck have you been ignoring me, Maxwell?" she asked hostilely.

If I'd thought she might've calmed down in the hours that had passed, her usage of my full first name cleared things up for me quickly.

"I wasn't ignoring you. I was asleep, and - "

"Asleep? Asleep when? I know *damn well* you ain't sleeping in your own bed because I sat outside your house for hours waiting on you to show up! Where are you?" she asked aggressively.

"Did you call me to fight? Because if you did, I don't got time for that shit," I said, preparing to hang up.

"I *called* to make sure your black ass was still alive and hadn't done nothing stupid, especially since the police are looking for you. Guess I was stupid to be concerned about you though because - "

"Wait, back up. Did you say the cops are looking for me?" I asked, locking eyes with Sophia. She hadn't really been paying attention to my conversation with Lilliana, but mentioning the law had her ears up.

"While I was sitting in front of your building, some detective asked if I knew you, and if you were home," Lilliana replied.

"And what did you say?" I asked, irritated by the pregnant pause in her speech.

"What the fuck do you think I said? Why would I lie about something that's easy to prove?"

"Okay, so what was the cop's name, and what *exactly* did he say?" I asked patiently.

"His name is Brewer, and all he said was that he needed to talk to you. What the fuck have you done now, Max?"

I hadn't done anything, but the fact that the same detective who had questioned me earlier was looking for me didn't give me the warm and fuzzies of an innocent man.

"Where are you now?" I asked.

"At the hospital, where *you* should be."

"What happened? Is-is my mom all right?" I asked, gripped by sudden fear.

"Nothing happened, I just came by to check on her. She's still in the ICU, but she's awake and asking for you."

"I'll be there in fifteen minutes," I replied, hanging up before she could start grilling my ass again.

"Everything good?" Sophia asked.

"Yes and no. My mom is awake and wanting to see me, but the cop who caught her shooting case was at my house looking for me."

"I know your mom didn't snitch on you. Maybe he's just doing a routine follow-up," Sophia said optimistically.

"Yeah, maybe, or he could be playing pin the tail on the donkey. Either way, I doubt I can avoid him for long, at least not without attracting suspicion. Right now I've gotta get to the hospital. Do you care if I leave this here?" I asked, pointing towards the backpack.

"Of course not. That'll give you a reason to come back when your girl asks."

"I don't need a reason. I'm a grown-ass man," I replied defiantly.

My statement made Sophia laugh, but I could tell that she liked what I'd said. When I scanned through my missed calls, I saw that all of them were from Lilliana, but that didn't surprise me. What *did* surprise me was the notification about a local news story talking about five bodies that were found in a dope house on the North side of the city.

"What the fuck," I mumbled in disbelief.

"Now what?"

"Pull out your phone and see if anything jumps out at you," I replied sarcastically.

While she did that, I read about how local law enforcement found five people dead from an apparent overdose in a house that was long suspected as a place where drugs were sold. The victims overdosing would've been considered just another statistic and sad situation in the hood, except all the victims were bound and gagged. That allowed the cops to conclude that the lethal blast they took wasn't voluntary, and that made it murder. When I finished reading the article, I looked up to find Sophia staring at me. The fact that she appeared completely emotionless to the situation didn't bother me. Her look of surprise did.

"So, is this what you meant when you said Lydia wouldn't have to worry about her nigga no more?" I asked, fighting to keep my voice calm.

"It had to be done."

"It had to be *done*? Are you serious right now, that's your response to this bullshit?" I asked angrily.

"It's the truth, Max, and you've been in this game long enough to know that. It wouldn't have taken long for them niggas to figure out that it was someone in their circle who betrayed them, and when they leaned on her, she would've given me up."

"Do you think the cops ain't gonna lean on her motherfucking ass? The fact that they're looking for me could mean she's already folded like a cheap suit!" I replied, becoming angrier with each passing moment.

"The cops bring a different kind of pressure, and she can stand that. Besides, she don't know you. I got this under control."

"Even if that's true, Sophia, when the fuck did we start lying to each other? I mean, damn, you know I'ma ride with you on whatever regardless, so you didn't have to keep me in the dark about what your play was," I said, involving some calm into my voice. I could tell by the immediate change in her facial expression that she felt bad for keeping that secret from me, and that made the situation we were in a little easier to deal with.

"No more lies," I said.

"No more lies," she agreed readily, leaning across the table and sealing her promise with a quick kiss.

Despite my body's desire to indulge in another round with Sophia, I kept my mind focused on what my next move should be. The first thing I did was send Lilliana a text telling her that it would be longer than fifteen minutes before I got to the hospital, but I was *definitely* coming.

"We need a plan," I said, stating the obvious.

"No matter what happens, we *never* admit to being in that house, and you gotta make sure your mom backs our story."

"I don't see why they would question my mom about that situation. She wasn't - "

Suddenly the answer to my own statement dawned on me.

"Her blood was on the floor," I whispered.

Sophia nodded her head, indicating that we were on the same page.

"Okay, I'll talk to my mom, and you just lay low," I said, standing up.

"Uh, we've got one more problem though."

"What?" I asked reluctantly.

"Lydia. Given everything that happened, it's too risky to keep her around. I gotta kill her."

ASAD

Chapter 5

I half expected to see Fayetteville cops waiting for me at the hospital, but when I arrived at the ICU wing, I only found Lilliana's disapproving stare.

"I see you found time to shower. Did Sophia join you?" she asked with obvious attitude.

"You can take that bullshit somewhere else because we're not doing this here. This hospital ain't big enough for your motherfucking insecurities."

"Insecurities? What the fuck am I supposed to think when you have me drop you off at that bitch's house and then you don't answer your phone for damn near eight hours? What would *you* think?" she asked, jumping up from her seat and getting in my face. Her attitude and tone made me wanna back hand the spit out of her mouth, especially since she was adding to my stress level, but lucky for her, my mom taught me better. Plus it was definitely a bad idea to make a scene in a hospital.

"Pinky, I'm sorry, okay. There's a lot going on and I'm trying to hold it together," I said, pulling her into my arms.

She kept her body stiff for a few seconds, but eventually loosened up and hugged me back.

"I want to help you, baby, but you gotta *let* me," she replied softly.

I took a deep breath, happy that her erratic mood had changed again so I could focus on what was important.

"You *are* helping me simply by being here. Have you been in to see my mom?"

"Not since earlier. They said only immediate family can go in. I told them that I was carrying her first grandchild, but that only worked one time," she replied, looking up at me smiling.

"Wh-what did you say? You're pregnant?" I said weakly.

45

"You should see the look on your face right now. I'm *lying,* fool," she whispered, laughing.

I didn't find a damn thing funny, but I smiled anyway.

"Let me go check on my mom real quick, okay?"

"I'll be here waiting on you," she replied, letting me go.

"Me too," chimed a voice from behind me.

I turned around to find Detective Brewer leaning against the wall with a look of boredom etched in the lines of his face. I made sure to conceal my nervousness by kissing Lilliana slowly and thoroughly before heading in the direction of my mom's room. When Lilliana had told me that the good detective was looking for me earlier, I didn't have a clue as to what it could be about. After talking with Sophia, I was betting it had to do with my mom's blood being at the scene of the latest crime to rock our city. Him wanting to talk to me signaled only one thing in my mind. He'd already spoke to my mom. From outside her door it looked like she was asleep, but suddenly her eyes popped open and locked on me.

"Max," she said weakly, smiling at me.

"Hi, Mommy, how are you feeling?" I asked, quickly closing the distance between us and taking her hand.

"I feel like I've been shot," she replied, chuckling.

Her joke immediately wiped the smile off of my face.

"Too soon? I'm sorry, son, I was just trying to lighten the mood."

"I'm so sorry, Mom, I - "

"I know you're sorry, and we don't need to keep going over that. Like I told the detective earlier, if it wasn't for you, I would've bled to death," she said, giving me a knowing look.

"He questioned you?" I asked.

"Of course. He wanted to know what I'd seen before I was shot, and I told him the truth. All I remember seeing was the rock cooking at the end of my pipe, and then I was beyond this world and the trivial shit in it. I didn't even know there were other people in that house with me, let alone that they were killed."

"What else did Detective Brewer say?" I asked, pulling up a chair so I could sit next to her bed.

"Well, he really wanted to know where you found me, for some reason. I told him that I didn't remember, but I thought I'd made it home."

"I told him that I found you in the hallway of our building, which I'm sure he probably checked for blood," I said, shaking my head.

"It doesn't matter. It's never what you *think* you know, it's only what you can prove. The only thing that can be *proven* is that you saved my life, and I'm thankful for that, Max. I'm gonna do my best not to throw this second chance away, but I need your help."

"Anything, Mom," I replied immediately, bringing her hand to my lips and kissing it.

"No more enabling. We both know that I need to get help for my addiction, and I don't want you giving me any more money to get high with. I'm not blaming you for me being this way, but I need your help in the form of tough love. Can you do that for me?"

"Absolutely. I think we need an environment change to go along with that too," I said.

"That costs money and time, because if I'm gonna stop getting high, you're gonna stay out of the streets. You're too smart and you've got too much potential to waste it or die for a few dollars. We're both gonna change – together - understand?"

"I understand," I replied.

This wasn't the first time my mom had promised to change and get clean, but the look in her eyes this time was different.

I wanted to believe in her with all my heart, but until I saw proof, there would always be doubt lingering in the back of my mind.

"I know that I'm gonna have to show you with my actions and not just words, so as soon as I'm cleared to leave, I'll be going to an in-patient drug program," she declared.

"You're what?"

"You heard me, Maxwell. I'm going into a drug program and it's sixty days long. After that, I'll be going to NA meetings every week, as many times a week as I need. I'll always be an addict, but I wanna be a *recovering* addict," she replied sincerely.

Hearing her plan had me completely blown away, almost to the point of tears, but I kept my emotions in check.

"I support you, Mom, and I'm proud of you," I said, kissing her hand again.

"Thank you. Now make me proud of you."

I didn't have to ask what she meant because the look she was giving me was clear.

"It's time to let your mom rest," Nurse Megan said from the doorway.

"I'll be back to see you in the morning, okay? I love you," I said, standing up and leaning over to kiss her on the forehead.

"I'll be here. Oh, and just because you've got the apartment to yourself tonight don't mean you can fuck your little girlfriend all over the place. Keep that shit in your room," she instructed.

"*Mom*," I said, embarrassed and shaking my head.

"You heard me. Now go."

I kissed her again before turning to leave, catching the smile that Megan couldn't hide quickly enough.

"She'll have her own room tomorrow, barring any setbacks," Megan informed me.

"Thank you for taking care of her."

"My pleasure," Megan replied, smiling.

I walked past her and out of the room, feeling a little better now that I'd actually seen my mom awake. I'd always thought that she was too damn stubborn to die, and I'd never been happier to be right than I was in this moment. I knew I couldn't bask in my feelings of gratefulness though because as promised, Detective Brewer was right where I left him, and clearly he wanted answers.

"How is she?" Lilliana asked, standing up as I came back into the waiting room.

"As good as can be expected. Definitely still a livewire," I replied, ignoring the look Brewer was leveling at me.

"Did you two get your stories straight?" he asked sarcastically.

"If you thought that there was a story that needed to be rehearsed, you wouldn't have let me go in there to see her without talking to me again first. So save your smart-ass comments and tell me what you want," I replied, annoyed.

"I suggest that you remember who you're talking to, kid, or you might find out how my kind gets down first hand," he threatened, smiling without a trace of humor.

It would've been incredibly stupid to gun down a cop in a hospital with cameras and witnesses everywhere, but I was still wishing that I had a gun right now.

"What do you want?" I asked through gritted teeth.

"I wanna talk about the job you pulled earlier," he replied, moving closer towards me.

"What's he talking about, Max?" Lilliana asked, looking at me with eyes drowning in terror.

Despite understanding that sometimes I had to do whatever was clever to make ends meet, me being locked up was her second biggest fear. Me dying was her first. My automatic response was to act completely and utterly ignorant, but there was a certainty in his eyes that translated into his words. I didn't know how much he knew, but I didn't feel like this nigga was on a fishing expedition. He knew *something*.

"Max, what is he - "

"Go outside, Lilliana. I'll meet you at my car," I said, looking at the detective closer. When she didn't immediately move towards the exit, I gave her a look that let her know that arguing right now would be foolish. After she reluctantly took the hint and left the waiting area, I nodded towards the semi-comfortable chairs that occupied the room, and we sat down side by side.

"I went to your apartment building," he said, breaking the silence first.

"And?"

"And I didn't find a droplet of fresh blood in the building or along the path that your mom would've taken to get there, but I'm sure you knew I wouldn't. Just like I'm sure that you know that I *did* find a lot of her blood in a trap house on the Northside, along with five dead bodies," he replied, calmly.

"I don't see how I would know *any* of that."

"Don't insult my intelligence, Max. Or should I call you Mad Max? That's what the streets call you, right? Well, Mad Max, I didn't get my detective's badge in the bottom of a Fruit Loops box or as a Happy Meal prize. I *earned* it, and part of that journey involves forming relationships with all different types of people, especially those who are 'bout that life. Forming those bonds makes my job infinitely easier at times because it allows me to put my ear to the streets and get results quickly. I wasn't surprised to find out about your alter ego as Mad Max. You come off as a good kid that gets good grades in school, and you will one day make something great of yourself. Beneath the surface there's more though, ain't it, Maxwell? Oh yeah, there's more to you than meets the eye. You've earned quite a rep to be as young as you are, and you've somehow managed to earn the respect of some of the heavy hitters out here. That job you pulled today though, that charged shit, and it might not be for the good. See, having a rep as a hustler is one thing, but the reputation of a killer can, and will, get you killed."

"I keep telling you that I don't know what - "

"It's the only thing that makes sense, Max. I admit, I don't know who shot your mom, but I know that the only way you could've saved her is if you were in that house. And if you were in that house, it damn sure wasn't to cop your morning fix," he said.

Right about now would be the time when all types of alarms and panic bells would start screaming in a nigga's brain because this cop was basically telling me that he could put me at the scene of a multiple homicide. Sure, it was only circumstantial, but a jury could draw the same conclusion and burn my black ass like bad chicken. The only thing that kept me from panicking was the fact that we weren't having this conversation in a police station after my rights had been read to me.

"If you believe that's true, why are we having this little talk?" I asked.

"To be honest, because I see a lot of myself in you, but I can tell by the talk we had earlier that you don't see the bigger picture."

"And what would that be?" I asked, hoping that the sarcasm I felt wasn't coming out with my words.

"We'll get to that in time, but for now, we need to address the bigger problem. Those niggas that died in that trap house have friends - powerful friends. The type of friends that you don't want as enemies, and when they find out that you took their money and product, they'll wanna talk to you."

The time for bullshitting, like I had no idea what he was talking about, had come and gone because we both knew what he meant when he said that them niggas' friends would want to *talk* to me.

"You don't strike me as the type to do favors, so what's this warning gonna cost me?" I asked.

"The warning is free, but there is a cost to do business."

"Hypothetically speaking, I'm thinking about a career change anyway, so the cost of doing business is an avoidable one for me," I said.

"Thinking about a career change is good, but you're not naïve enough to believe that you can leave the game behind. You gotta know that you're in way too deep now," he replied seriously, looking at me.

The kid in me wanted to protest, but the hustler in me knew that I'd been playing a grown man's game for a while. Today's activities had taken me from high school straight to the NBA, and it was too soon to retire.

"So what do you suggest?" I asked.

"I suggest that you prepare mentally to rise to the occasion, because it's only gonna get realer from here. You can be richer and more powerful than any kingpin that you can think of, but only if you can admit one thing to yourself."

"Admit what?" I asked, confused.

"Admit that you want it. That you want that life and all that comes with it. To survive and have longevity, you have to commit early on to doing shit the right way and not halfway, because it's all or nothing at this point. So what do you want?"

Following his question, I could see myself in my mind's eye standing in front of an open door, but all I could see was darkness. The question Detective Brewer was asking was would I walk through that door into the darkness and all the unknown that came with it? For this question to be coming from him told me that there was obviously more unknown than I'd considered for my life, but it didn't change the truth of me being in too deep to turn back.

"I want it. I want it all. So what do I gotta do next?"

ASAD

Chapter 6
One week later

"When are you gonna tell me why we're making this long-ass drive to Virginia?" Sophia asked, yawning and trying to get comfortable in the passenger seat of the sports car I was navigating.

"I already told you, we're meeting someone," I replied.

"My nigga, you *know* I trust you, but all this vague shit you've been on lately is a bit much. Why are you being so secretive all of a sudden?"

Sophia's loyalty would never be in question with me, and I knew eventually I'd have to give her answers, but I still hadn't figured out what exactly to tell her. The last week had been one of the craziest in my young life, and not just because I was fucking two women I genuinely cared about. True enough, I'd never seen myself as being *that* guy, but Sophia and Lilliana played different, yet equally important, positions in my life. With my mom still in the hospital recovering, Lilliana had turned into a housewife, not leaving my side even when her father demanded that she come home. Sophia, on the other hand, had become as necessary in the streets by my side as my heart beating in my chest in terms of survival. After doing a little research of my own, I'd learned that Detective Brewer wasn't lying about the new enemies I'd inherited courtesy of Sophia's shenanigans. That made my decision about early retirement easier, and opened the door for Brewer and me to have some real talk. All my life I'd thought of crooked cops as the white dudes I saw on TV getting away with hurting and killing minorities, along with the black cops who had the slave mentality. Detective Brewer didn't fit in either box though. He was simply a nigga from the slums who was about his money, and having a badge made it easier to earn. He presented himself as a modern day Robin Hood who took from the undeserving and gave back to those he cared about. The opportunity he'd offered me was something like a paid apprenticeship, and in the last seven days, I'd done a lot of on the job training.

The jet black 2008 AMG 55 Benz coupe I was driving was just the latest example of my training because I'd put two Glock .40's in a dopeboy's face and made him find other transportation home. This was actually my third carjacking of the week, netting me a quick sixty thousand dollars after cutting Sophia in for thirty thousand. I knew good money wasn't gonna stop her from asking questions, but I hadn't figured out how to explain the police angel. We were taking the Benz to Virginia so it could be put in a shipping container and shipped abroad, and there was no way I could avoid giving her answers for the next four hours.

"I know I've been slick ducking your questions, but that's because I really don't know how to explain the situation to you," I confessed.

"Just say whatever it is you gotta say. It ain't like it's gonna change shit between me and you."

Her statement caused me to look over at her, finding her curled up in the plush leather seat facing me with a sincere expression riding her beautiful features in the moonlight's glow.

"I'm not so sure about that, but our relationship ain't never been built on secrets. We've been on some real 'get money' shit this week, which ain't nothing out of the ordinary, but I know you noticed that shit is more organized now and I've only been working with you," I said.

"I noticed, and I'm not complaining."

"Well, things have changed because I've got a new partner, of sorts."

"Boy, stop dancing and get to the damn point," she said impatiently.

"I got a cop feeding me info about what jobs to pull and who to pull them on," I blurted out.

When I looked over at her I expected to find a look of judgement or disbelief, but instead, Sophia actually looked bored. "A cop? Okay, and?" she asked.

"What do you mean and? I thought you would be tripping about me fucking with the law."

"You trippin'. Every major player has cops on their payroll, so the fact that you've now got one means you're elevating your level of play in the fame. I just appreciate you bringing me along for the ride," she replied honestly.

Surprise couldn't begin to describe how I felt now, but what she said made perfect sense. I'd been looking at it like a li'l nigga scrambling for pocket change, but this move could put me in the arena with the bosses. Detective Brewer had told me as much, but it was different when I heard it from someone I knew and trusted with my life.

"You already know that there's no one I trust more than you in these streets, so of course you gotta be by my side with this next step. Your ass just better not kill nobody else without running it past me first!" I warned.

"Well, with your new connections we're untouchable anyway, so - "

"That's the exact wrong attitude to take, Sophia. You don't know it, but that shit you did came with some heavy consequences because them niggas was connected to some people in Miami. Them people got a long reach."

"Lydia was the only loose end, and I took care of that so nothing would've blown back on us anyway," she replied defensively.

"You telling me what you *think*, but I'm telling you what I *know*. Just because there were no witnesses don't mean that don't nobody know nothing because the streets is *always* watching. Trust me."

The little space between us quickly filled with awkward silence and I knew she was feeling some type of way about my criticism of her decision. That didn't make me want to take back anything I'd said though. We needed to get an understanding because the future looked too bright to let it slip through our grasp on some nonsense. I didn't like the silence, but I continued to drive while being determined not to break it because I'd meant what I said.

"I won't kill anyone without your approval unless I have to, as in a life or death situation," she conceded after five minutes of heavy breathing.

"Thank you. I'm not trying to be hard on you or tell you how to live your life, but I want to see you win in this game just like me. I feel like the potential for the future is limitless if we play it right."

"I'm with you no matter what. How much does Lilliana and your mom know though?" she asked.

"Lilliana don't know shit except that I'm not going to jail, and as for my mom…"

I let my sentence trail off because I'd already filled Sophia in on my mom's demands for my future. I believed she wanted the best for me, but the reality that she didn't want to accept was that a beautiful future would only be earned by doing some ugly shit. I was determined not to use the environment I was born into as an excuse for why I wouldn't succeed in life.

"Based on what you told me, I doubt your mom would change her mind, even if she knew you were big time now," Sophia replied.

"I'm not big time yet, but you're probably right. This has to stay between us, okay?"

"Understood. So, are we really just driving way out here to meet someone?" she asked.

"Yeah, we're dropping this car off and picking another one up. You're driving back though because I'm already tired as fuck."

"You should've told Lilliana to let you get some sleep last night," she replied sarcastically.

"Whatever, smart ass, I didn't even have sex with her last night, so cut your shit."

"You don't owe me no explanations. That's your wifey, so you can do whatever you wanna do with her."

"I know that, and I ain't never needed your permission to get my dick wet before. Has that changed now that I'm sticking my dick in you?" I asked, cutting my eyes in her direction.

"Nah, my nigga, you good."

In no way did her words match the expression on her face, which made it obvious we were gonna clear the air on all things during this road trip. I didn't know that I was ready for all that, but I cared about Sophia too much to ignore her feelings.

"You know it ain't just sex between us, right?" I asked softly.

Her response was to turn the radio on and crank the volume up, but I refused to feed into her immaturity or avoid the elephant in the car with us, so I shut it off just as quick.

"I was being serious, Sophia. You mean more to me than some sweat in the sheets."

"I'm your best friend, I get it," she replied.

"Yeah, you are, and that makes our physical connection deeper than the average. I know it wasn't planned, and it started in a moment of high emotion, but I don't have any regrets. Do you?"

She was quiet just long enough to have me wondering if she truly felt like she made a mistake.

"No, I don't have any regrets, but I do have feelings," she replied vulnerably.

"I know that, and I'll do my best to protect them, but I need to know what you expect of me."

"Honestly, brutal honesty," she replied without hesitation.

I opened my mouth to quickly assure her that nothing would change with us when it came to that because I always kept shit fifty with her, but looking at her, I realized she meant something different.

"Brutal honesty, huh? Okay. I love you too," I said.

"But you're in love with her, right?" she asked, smiling sadly.

"I don't know the answer to that question, I mean, I'm only sixteen. I think I'm mature for my age, but I ain't 'bout to get married no time soon. Right now Lilliana and I are playing house, but that don't mean I can't see a life with you, especially given our similarities."

"So in the meantime, you just plan to keep fucking both of us?" she asked.

"Yeah."

My reply made her laugh instantly, which caught me off guard.

"Well, I did ask for brutal honesty. Just make sure you wear a condom from now on," she said, shaking her head as she pulled out a pre-rolled blunt and lit it.

"Yo, we can't deliver the car smelling like weed," I said.

"Relax, we've still got a long way to go, and I'll let the window down."

I knew any further argument would be a waste of time so I kept my mouth shut until she passed me that blunt to slide in between my lips. With the serious conversations out of the way she turned the music back on, and we kept pushing up the highway under the haze of some good hydro.

A couple hours later, Sophia thought it was a good idea to give me head while I drove, which almost caused me to put us in a ditch on the side of the road. I managed to fight through though and before I knew it, I was parking at the rest stop rendezvous outside of Norfolk, Virginia. Thankfully we only had to wait a few minutes before a yellow 2008 Lamborghini Gallardo Snyder pulled up next to us.

"Damn, I'm driving *that*?" Sophia asked in awe.

"You gotta be kidding me," I said, opening my door and hopping out for a closer inspection.

I don't know who I was expecting to step out of the Lambo, but it damn sure wasn't the white guy in the tailored blue suit making his way towards me. He had the look of a banker or somebody who worked on Wall Street, not someone who got down like Sophia and I.

"Keys?" he asked.

"In the car," I replied.

"Me too. I was told to tell you that you'll be met at the North Carolina state line, and you're to head straight back," he said, moving past me and climbing behind the wheel of the Benz.

Without delay, he pulled off into the night.

"Hold up, Negro, you said I was driving back," Sophia reminded me. I hadn't realized I was moving towards the driver's side door until her statement stopped me in my tracks.

"I mean, I did say that, but - "

"Nah, no buts, get your ass in," she said, rushing to the open car door and throwing herself behind the wheel.

Something in me told me that if I tried protesting, I'd be doing it to the rearview lights, so I got in the car. Before I could put my seatbelt on, I was pinned to the seat as she gunned the engine and we squealed off into the night.

"Slow down," I demanded.

"You just jealous that your ass ain't pushing this bad mu'fucka, so shut up and ride or I'ma drop the top in this motherfucker," she threatened, ripping through gears like a professional race car driver.

After getting my seatbelt securely fastened I did like I was told, but I was praying every time as we vanished into the night. I'd never doubted Sophia's driving abilities, but I knew real fear for our first few hours on the road because the speedometer hovered around 140 mph. Finally I was able to close my eyes and find the land of sleep, but it felt like as soon as it got good, I was snatched back to consciousness.

"What is it?" I asked, feeling Sophia nudge me awake. Before she could utter a word I took in the flashing blue lights and the fact that we were on the side of the road.

"I told you to slow the fuck down," I said angrily, checking my side mirror.

"Now ain't the time for I told you so," she replied, carefully and slowly pulling her pistol from the waist of her jeans.

The metallic sound of her chambering a bullet made her intentions clear.

"Calm down, Sophia, it's only a ticket. I'm pretty sure this car has legit plates and a clean VIN number, and there's no probable cause to search us, so just chill."

The look she gave me told me that she'd rather shoot it out, but she reluctantly slid the gun under her right leg where she could still get to it.

"You better hope you're right because if he says step out of the car, I'm dropping him where he stands."

ASAD

Chapter 7

I knew that she meant what she said, but dropping a cop was bad no matter who you had on the payroll. In this moment I also knew that we had limited options, but instead of reaching for my own gun, I pulled out my phone out and sent a quick text.

"Getting us a lawyer?" Sophia asked sarcastically, checking her side mirror as nonchalantly as she could.

I ignored her comment and waited with baited breath in hopes that Brewer would answer my message immediately.

"Why ain't the cop get out of the car yet?" she asked after a long two minutes.

"I was just wondering the same thing. Odds are they're either running the plates, or waiting for backup because it's after two in the morning."

"Calling for backup is bad for us, Max, real bad. I say we just make a run for it."

"Stating the obvious ain't helping our situation, and if we were gonna make a run for it, why the fuck did you pull over?" I asked with growing frustration.

"It seemed like a good idea at the time, goddammit, but if you want me to take off, I will," she replied heatedly, reaching for the emergency brake.

Movement in my side mirror caught my attention, and hers as well, and what we saw wasn't good.

"That ain't a regular cop. That's a Virginia state trooper," Sophia said softly.

Suddenly my phone vibrated in my hand and for a moment I felt relief, but that moment was short-lived because our situation went from bad to worse.

"Oh God," I sighed.

"What, what's wrong?"

"There's dope in the car," I replied, fighting against the panic in my chest.

"You've gotta be bullshitting. Where and how much?"

"I don't know, all I was told is that there's dope in the car and under *no* circumstances am I to let it get seized," I replied, locking eyes with her.

"Fuck it, let's - "

Whatever idea Sophia was about to suggest she had to swallow because the state trooper was tapping on the driver's side window with his Maglite. The look in her eyes was asking me a question that I honestly didn't have the answer to.

"Just be cool," I whispered.

"Good evening, Officer," she said once she'd rolled the window down.

"License and registration," came a voice with a harsh country twang.

Deep down we both knew how this was likely to play out if we didn't change the course of events, and the anticipation of the next few minutes had my stomach in knots. When Sophia leaned over to get the car's registration from the glove box, I discreetly slid the pistol from beneath her leg and under mine.

"What the fuck?" she whispered furiously.

"Trust me," I mumbled.

Her eyes held a hint of uncertainty, but unless she was gonna make a scene, she didn't have any other option except to follow my lead. She handed the requested documents out the window, and to both of our dismay, the cop didn't even look at them.

"Step out of the car, ma'am," the cop demanded immediately.

"Wh-what for? What have I done wrong?" Sophia asked.

"Ma'am, you need to step out of the car," the cop replied, backing up and resting his hand on the butt of his gun.

The threat was obvious, and that made my decision for me.

"Don't argue, just do it," I whispered.

Her movements were reluctant, but she slowly opened the door and stepped out of the car, shielding me from the cop's view long enough for me to grab the pistol and fire two shots as soon as she wasn't in the way. The roar of the 9mm Glock echoed far off into the night, but I was only concerned with making sure my target stayed down. I quickly scrambled out of the passenger side and ran around the car until I was looming over top of the fallen trooper. My shots had caught him in the chest and taken him off of his feet, but I could see the bulletproof vest poking through his ruined uniform.

"Please, please, I have - "

A well-placed head shot ended his begging and his life, and I didn't have time to question or analyze my decision.

"Get back in the car. I'll follow you," I said.

"You can't take the cop car, it's got a GPS locator on it."

"It's also got a dash cam that caught all of this, so it has to be destroyed. We'll get away from here. You go to a gas station and buy a gas can, fill it up, and we'll find somewhere to burn it," I replied.

Sophia nodded her head, grabbed her license and registration off the ground, and got back behind the wheel. I ran to the cop car, got in, and peeled off after her. Like a song stuck in my head all I kept asking myself was what had I done? Self-preservation was undoubtedly what I'd done, but that didn't make it right or any easier to accept. I knew in the days to come I'd rationalize and tell myself over and over that I hadn't had a choice, but that would just be a lie I told myself. I'd had a choice, and now I'd rung a bell that I couldn't unring. It took us fifteen minutes to find a gas station, and then we had to park down the street so Sophia could go on foot.

"Take this, and hurry up," I said, passing her my gun.

We shared a brief kiss before she took off, and then I was left alone to figure out what the next series of moves would be. I knew what I had to do first and I immediately got to it by retrieving my phone off of the passenger side floor of the Lambo. Despite it being the middle of the night, Detective Brewer answered on the second ring, and without a hint of sleep in his voice.

"You got some motherfucking explaining to do," I said hostilely.

"I probably do, but I hope you're smart enough to know that this ain't a conversation for an open phone line. Where are you?"

"I stopped for fucking ice cream. I'll be there in two hours," I replied, hanging up angrier than when I'd called.

I was really contemplating putting a much-needed bullet in Brewer's head when I saw his sneaky ass because his bullshit could've lost me or Sophia our lives or freedom. True enough, I'd agreed to do business with the deal, but life and death surprises weren't part of that deal and we were gonna get that shit straight ASAP. For the longest ten minutes of my life my mind raced in wild thoughts ranging from me getting caught in the immediate future with this dead cop's car to Sophia just walking away and leaving me to clean up this mess. If she did, I wouldn't have blamed her because it was my fault she was in this shit, but thankfully she emerged from the shadows in time to prevent my nervous breakdown.

"Where are we going to burn it?" she asked, holding up the gas can.

I had no idea where we were, for real. I only knew the exit we'd taken and that we were still in Virginia. Looking around, all I saw were warehouse buildings in one direction and rolling fields in another. One thing I knew with absolute certainty was that if I got caught driving this car, I'd definitely be on death row by next Tuesday.

"Fuck it, we burn it here," I replied, taking the can from her and getting to work. Within minutes we had a roaring bonfire type blaze and I was behind the wheel of the Lambo getting us the fuck out of Dodge.

"You okay?" Sophia asked thirty minutes later.

I wasn't sure how to answer that question. All I knew was that something in me had allowed me to set all emotion aside for the moment. I'd never considered myself a sociopath, but right now I wasn't feeling remorse for what I'd done.

"Yeah, I'm good. How 'bout you?" I asked, looking over at her.

"Honestly I could care less about a cop losing his life. They signed up for that shit. I just don't get why you had to do it when I would've done it, and it would've been cleaner because we would've still been in the car."

"I was trying to avoid it all together, Sophia, but shit got out of control too fast for me to stop it," I replied.

"I need you to be honest with me. Did you really not know that there was dope in this car?"

"Of course I didn't know, or I would've told you. I definitely wouldn't have let you drive because it would've been my responsibility to make sure the delivery took place without any problems," I replied.

"Then we need to have a long talk with your man, because ―"

"No, I need to have a long talk with him. The less you know, the less of a threat you can pose to him."

"I don't see how we're gonna avoid me meeting him, considering we're gonna be met at the state line," she said logically.

"I know what I'm doing; just trust me," I replied.

Silence followed my statement, but it didn't make me feel like Sophia was doubting me. It wasn't my intention to shut her out because I'd meant what I'd told her earlier about needing her, and trusting *only* her. I had to protect her though because right now, I wasn't one hundred percent convinced that I could or should trust Detective Brewer. Until I figured that out, I'd have to be the only one on the front line next to him. I knew which route he'd be expecting me to take to get back to North Carolina, which was why I made a slight detour. It added an extra forty-five minutes to the journey, but it was worth it to get Sophia home safe.

"You sure you wanna go at this alone?" she asked once I pulled up in front of her apartment building.

"It's the smart play. I'll be back after I get this car dropped off. I'll even bring you some breakfast."

"Bribery will get you nowhere. Besides, I'd rather eat you for breakfast," she replied, giving me a quick kiss before climbing out of the car.

Once she'd disappeared from view, I pulled out my phone to text Brewer. Not surprisingly, there were a few texts from him asking for my location, each one expressing more concern than the previous one. I'd felt my phone vibrating when I'd been driving, and I'd had no doubt about who it was trying to contact me, but he deserved to sweat. I sent him a text letting him know that I was back in town, and asked where he wanted to meet up. Within seconds he'd texted me a familiar address that caused a knot to return to the pit of my stomach. No delay would change what was to come though, so I pointed the car in the right direction and got on my way. Fifteen minutes later,

I pulled into the parking spot next to my navy blue box Chevy, grabbed Sophia's pistol, and got out of the car.

"You're late," Detective Brewer said, calmly taking in the sight of the pistol, but not flinching in the slightest.

"Yeah, I had some car trouble."

"Nothing you couldn't handle, I see," he said, nodding his head with obvious approval while still leaning up against my car.

"Maybe I'm not done handling it," I replied, clutching the gun in my hand tighter as anger flooded my veins.

"Easy, Mad Max, before you make a mistake that you'll regret forever."

"You didn't think I've already done that tonight because of your bullshit?" I asked heatedly.

"No, I think you did what you had to do, and it was the right thing. Trust me."

"*Trust* you? Trust *you*? My nigga, you *really* didn't just say those two words to me," I said, closing the distance between us and pushing the barrel of the pistol into his stomach.

To my amazement, my actions made him smile, but I didn't let them disarm me or make me lower the gun.

"You think that gun you've got jammed in my stomach scares me? It don't. It *excites* me because it only further proves that I was right about you. When you looked me in my eyes and told me that you wanted this life, and everything in it, I believed you. I could feel the desire in you. The only question was would you do what was absolutely necessary to obtain the dream you're chasing."

"So you lied and sent me on a dummy mission," I said, becoming angrier with each passing second.

"I didn't send you on a dummy mission, Maxwell, I just tested you. I put you in a life or death situation *knowing* that you would choose you and your girlfriend's lives over anyone else's ten out of ten times. Did you really think that I could give you the game without being one hundred percent convinced that you were ready for it?"

I had to take a few deep breaths before speaking because the screaming in my mind was threatening to overtake me. I was trying not to show my shock over the fact that he somehow knew about Sophia, and at the same time, my mind was circling around what else he'd said. A test? Did he actually think that what he'd done was okay?

"You know that I don't have a problem blowing your stomach through your spine, right?" I asked calmly.

"I know, but you'd lose more than you stand to gain. What happened tonight was a one-time thing because I'm completely convinced that you're ready for the next step. I especially like how you managed to stay calm enough to get your girl to safety before meeting me. That shows your loyalty to me and to her, and that's not something a lot of people could pull off. I'm proud of you."

I knew that anyone else in my situation would've thought Brewer was being condescending, but that wasn't what I got from his tone. This shit wasn't a game to him, despite how everything we did was characterized in the streets, and I respected that.

"So now what?" I asked, lowering the gun and stepping back.

"Now we break bread. Grab the duffle bag out of the trunk and let's step into your apartment."

I did as instructed, making sure to scan my surroundings because you never knew who was lurking in the projects. With the bag in hand I led the way upstairs to the apartment I shared with my mom, pushing aside the guilt I felt about bringing dope across her threshold. Thankfully she wasn't home to witness this. I set the bag on the kitchen table and Brewer immediately unzipped it, pulling out its contents. With each brick he put on the table my eyes got bigger and my stomach got weaker, but I kept my mouth shut until he looked at me.

"You know what this is?" he asked.

"Looks like cocaine."

"Maybe, but it's not. It's that boy known as heroin, and right now it's worth more than coke per key," he said.

"I told you before that I don't sell drugs."

"And I told you when I met you that your rep as a hustler is solid. That means you'll find a way to make it work. You've got a month to move all five of these keys, and if you can do that, then the world is yours. Don't disappoint me."

ASAD

Chapter 8

"You promised me breakfast," Sophia said sleepily, turning away from her open door and walking back into her apartment.

"I brought you something better than breakfast."

"Dick at sunrise is good, but I'd just made it to sleep before you started banging on my door and now I want that more than dick. So if you ain't got no food in that bag, you can wake me up in a few hours," she said, crawling her beautiful naked ass back beneath her comforter. As soon as I'd come through the door and shut it I smelled the weed in the air, and the further I moved inside the apartment, the stronger the aroma.

"Smells like you're baking weed brownies, I commented, noticing the half pound of bud on her kitchen table.

"Just trying to relax."

I knew her well enough to know that what she'd smoked in the hour I'd been gone wasn't about unwinding. It was purely stress-related. That made me question whether or not I should bring her along for this ride but the truth was that I needed her too much to turn back. Without a word I walked over to her bed, opened the duffle bag, and dumped the contents on the mattress next to her. When she turned her head to look, I saw the tiredness vanish as she quickly sat up.

"Is that what I think it is?" she asked slowly.

"If you're thinking its coke, it's not. It's heroin. Ninety-seven percent pure heroin, worth about forty thousand dollars a key before it's stepped on, and at least double that if you cut it right."

"When the fuck did you become an expert on heroin?" she asked, picking up a brick and inspecting it with the carefulness of a new mother.

"I'm not an expert. I'm simply repeating what was told to me after it was given to me."

"Given to you? Is this what was stashed in the car?" she asked in disbelief.

"Uh huh."

"Max, that's almost a quarter of a million in uncut dope, and he *gave* it to you?" she asked slowly, no longer studying the dope, but focusing intently on my face.

"He didn't give it to me like it's mine to have, but he's expecting me to move it. In a month."

"Five keys in a month? That nigga is trippin' and he's setting you up to fail because he knows you ain't in the dope game, which means you don't have the clientele to dump this shit like that," she replied, clearly frustrated.

"You're right, he knows I don't sell drugs, but he knows I'll rise to the challenge and make this shit disappear like Houdini."

"Okay, Houdini, what's your plan?" she asked.

The truth was that I hadn't formulated a clear plan yet, but I knew Sophia was more than capable of coming up with a way to make shit happen. I just had to let her think it was her idea.

"Why you staring at me like that?" she asked after a full minute of silence.

"Because you're naked."

"Nah, nigga, that ain't lust in your eyes, it's some sneaky shit," she insisted.

I ignored her accusations and suspicions while slowly taking my clothes off. She kept her eyes glued to my face for as long as she could, but eventually they moved lower until she was eye to eye with something she liked. I didn't move towards her like I knew she was anticipating. Instead, I grabbed my dick and began stroking it slowly. The way she licked her lips involuntarily told me that I had her mouth watering, and I was content to let the suspense build. I maintained the same steady pace, moving my hand back and forth until my dick was hard enough to hold up a high rise building.

"You think you gonna make me beg for it?" she asked softly.

"Maybe."

The wicked smile she gave me should've been warning enough, but I still wasn't prepared for her to kick her comforter to the floor and get on her hands and knees with her ass pointed at me.

"I won't beg, but you can stick it in whenever you like," she said seductively.

When I took that last step to bring me within inches of her, I knew that the hunter was in danger of becoming the hunted, but I still didn't touch her.

"You know you want it. All you gotta do is say so," I replied, equally seductive.

She didn't respond with words, but her actions were the equivalent of a mic drop. While looking back at me over her shoulder, she smiled and then reached in between her legs to use two fingers to spread her pussy lips open. Me leaning forward wasn't a conscious effort, but suddenly I felt the same shock of adrenaline as I would diving into a Jacuzzi. The drip her pussy put on me made it hard to breathe, but I wasn't about to stop or turn back. With a hand on each hip I pushed deeper inside her secret garden until every corner was explored, and only then did I retreat with the intentions of invading again. Our pace was slow at first, allowing us both to savor every stroke, but we understood that that could only last for so long. When she tooted her ass up further in the air, I tightened my grip on her while delivering blows that made her knees wobble.

"O-o-kay," she mumbled, trying to brace herself so she wouldn't go flying over the side of her bed. The way her plump ass cheeks bounced off my thighs only motivated me to increase the pressure behind my strokes, and within minutes, I felt her whole body rock with joy.

"M-max! I-I-I'm g-good," she stammered breathlessly.

That was the closest she'd ever come to surrendering to me, and that had me feeling myself on another level.

"Y-you want me to stop?" I asked while increasing both speed and force.

"Oh God!" she screamed.

"Yes or no?" I asked, punctuating each word with a pounding blow that made her toes curl.

"N-n-no!"

I knew I could've asked her the same question in a million different ways and she would've answered the same way every time. The time for talking was over though, and I would let my dick speak for itself. I rode her fast and then slow, bringing her right to the edge of complete fulfillment, but not letting her taste that dream. When I finally did let her cum the tide shifted, and she made me lay down so she could ride me. It took her three minutes at a full gallop to push my eyes into the back of my head as I lost my life inside her, spewing wave after wave in a blinding climax. It was still another half an hour before she climbed off of me, and by then I was too weak to talk, so we slept.

The sound of someone banging on her front door was what brought us back to consciousness.

"You expecting someone?" I asked, looking over at her.

"Nope," she replied, pulling a chrome .38 from under her pillow.

"Where's my gun?"

"Kitchen counter," she replied, getting out of bed and pulling on some shorts and a sports bra.

I only had time to put my boxers on before the pounding started again.

"Whoever that is really wants to talk to you."

"Goddammit, Max, I know you're in there!" Lilliana yelled.

"Nah, she wants to talk to *you*," Sophia said, smiling.

"Oh fuck," I murmured while quickly pulling on the rest of my clothes and heading for the door.

She had just started hammering on the door again when I snatched it open.

"What the fuck is wrong with you?" I asked angrily.

"What the fuck is wrong with *you*!" she exclaimed, pushing past me into the apartment.

"You trippin' and I ain't - "

"No, nigga, I ain't trippin'! I been calling your ass all motherfucking morning, but like always, you don't answer the phone when you're with your *other* bitch," Lilliana said, looking at Sophia like she was ready to snatch her wig.

I was sure the pistol in Sophia's hand was the only thing stopping her.

"I don't do domestic disputes," Sophia said calmly, wearing that same devilish smile.

"Lilliana, what's the real issue?" I asked, hoping to diffuse the situation.

"The problem is I don't like you being with her all the time, I don't like that you don't answer your phone when you're with her, and right now I don't like the way she's fucking looking at me," Lilliana replied, taking an aggressive step towards Sophia.

The sound of Sophia cocking the hammer on her pistol stopped any more forward progress though.

"Listen, we can discuss all this emotional shit later. Right now I got work to do," I said.

"Yeah, right, you probably just finished *working* that bitch! It smells like stank pussy in here," Lilliana spat, her eyes flaming with anger that was now turned on me.

I was about to flip all the way out on her ass, but I caught sight of the look on Sophia's face, which made me quickly put myself in between them.

"Chill," I said, gently putting a hand on Sophia's chest.

"You better get her the fuck out of here before I hurt her," Sophia warned in a deadly whisper.

"I ain't going no fucking where as long as my man is here, bitch!" Lilliana said from behind me.

I could tell by the look on Sophia's face that this shit was no longer a laughing matter, and we were only seconds away from things becoming too real to turn back.

"I'll be back in a little while and we'll figure out what to do. Just hold onto everything until then," I said, nodding towards the dope that was still on her bed.

"I got you, but - "

"Nigga, you won't be coming back here *no* time soon, so ain't no need giving her fake hope. She can find somebody else to get money with," Lilliana stated decidedly.

I turned around, intending to put Lilliana in her place, but Sophia's sudden laughter froze the words in my throat.

"Laugh all you want, bitch, I bet he don't come back," Lilliana said confidently.

"I'm not laughing at what you said. I'm laughing at the fact that you actually think you can tell Max what to do. It's obvious that you have no clue who your man is," Sophia replied.

"Max, tell this bitch you ain't rocking with her no more so we can get the fuck out of here. The smell is starting to give me a headache," Lilliana said, waving her hand back and forth in front of her nose for dramatic affect.

Again laughter from behind me stopped my reply, but this time there was no humor in it, and that gave me a bad feeling.

"Glad you think it's funny with your nasty - "

"It's funny because I know my pussy don't stink, but just in case I'm wrong, why don't you smell your man's dick and let me know," Sophia stated calmly.

If my reflexes weren't quick there was no way I would've been able to grab Lilliana before she got around me to Sophia, but thankfully I did.

"Put me the fuck down! I'ma beat that hoe!" Lilliana yelled, struggling like a wild cat in my arms.

"Chill the fuck out," I growled, carrying her through the open front door and out into the hallway.

The fact that Sophia was laughing again wasn't helping matters, and so even when I put Lilliana down I had to close the door to prevent her from going back inside.

"Why the fuck are you protecting that bitch, Max? Let me fuck her up!"

"It ain't about protecting her. This is about you bugging the fuck out for no reason. You can't just come to people's house and start poppin' shit because you in your feeling. That will get your ass shot," I replied, frustrated.

"Well I wouldn't have to pop up nowhere if you would answer your motherfucking phone, nigga! You answer anytime that bitch calls you, but I can't get the same respect? You must be fucking her then!"

"I ain't fucking nobody but you, so don't start - "

"Prove it. Pull your dick out and let me smell it," she demanded.

My first reaction was to laugh in her face, but I could tell that she was heart attack serious.

"Stop playing and just tell me what was so important that you had to track me down," I replied, trying to change the subject.

"We'll get to that in a second, but first I'ma need you to pull your dick out."

"I'm not pulling my dick out in a project hallway. Cut the jokes."

"This ain't no joke. If that bitch is lying, then you can prove that right here, right now. I'll even suck it for you when I'm done. If you're feeling that shy we can go to your car, but either way, you're gonna let me check your dick. Or else," she said, crossing her arms over her chest.

"Or else what? Look, girl, I told you I had shit to do, so if you gonna keep playing games, then you can leave."

"You think I'm playing with you, Maxwell? That bitch just said you fucked her, and instead of proving that she's lying, you're trying to turn it around on me?" she asked in disbelief.

I knew that I had to choose my words carefully at this point, but honestly, I didn't see no way out of this situation besides going on the offensive.

"I shouldn't have to prove shit. You should trust my word over anyone else's. Until you can do that, we ain't got shit to talk about."

With that said I opened the door to Sophia's apartment, walked in, and shut it without looking back. I half expected Lilliana to start banging again, but after thirty seconds of silence, I breathed a needed sigh of relief.

"You need to get your bitch in check because next time I won't be so nice," Sophia said from her seat at the kitchen table.

"I ain't even trying to talk about it. What are you doing?" I asked, moving towards her.

"What you wanted me to do. I'm making shit happen."

When I got to the table I saw that she had a kilo already open and she was breaking it down into ounces.

"You got something lined up?" I asked.

"I made a few calls while you were talking with your wife, and there's some interest, but we gotta talk numbers. How much is he expecting you to bring back?"

"Two hundred thousand, no less," I replied.

"So he expects you to make all your profit off of the cut, even though he knows you don't sell dope? You sure he ain't setting you up for failure?"

"I'm sure. Besides, if this shit was easy, then everybody would do it. He knows the dope is good enough for e to get rid of it wholesale and have his money back to him in no time. Right now he's trying to see how resourceful I am. He's testing me, just like last night," I replied.

"Wait, what do you mean just like last night?"

I quickly relayed the conversation I'd had with Detective Brewer, and I could tell by the look on her face that she didn't like it one bit.

"Please tell me that you're not putting your trust into this sick motherfucker," she said when I was done talking.

"I told you, I trust you, and that's it right now."

"Which explains why you tried to fuck me real good, so I'd help you with this," she said, gesturing toward the piles of dope in front of her.

"Nah, I already knew that you would help, the sex was just an added bonus. So tell me what the play is."

"Well, I got a few people that want us to slide through so their testers can see what we got. Now that I know what the deal is, I guess I gotta cut this shit myself so we can get maximum return while creating a steady client list," she replied.

"You know how to cut heroin?"

"I learned a lot before I left home. Don't worry, I'll make this money, you just take care of me."

"Always," I promised.

Chapter 9
Three weeks later

"So what do you think?" I asked.

"I think it makes more sense to get a house for space reasons, but with an apartment, it's harder for cops to monitor the foot traffic," Sophia replied, passing me the lit blunt.

It wasn't a smart idea to be smoking on school property, but it was necessary that we talk, and I'd already missed more days than I liked. Besides, weed smoke was the least of the cops' worries at Westover high school.

"How many apartments you thinking?" I asked.

"Well, we got everything locked down from North to East through my people, so really all we need to do is set something up in the South. Maybe three spots at the most."

In the last three weeks I'd seen enough money to understand a dope boy's addiction, but I still wasn't getting my hands dirty. My job was to oversee the operation and count that money because it was my ass on the line for it. It had only taken two weeks to bring Brewer his money back, but that two weeks had been a lifetime education on how the dope game worked. Sophia had done as she promised and cut the heroin to where it was still lethal enough to smoke, but plentiful enough that we'd eat good. Our product swam through Fayetteville like a typhoon, even bringing in clients from South Carolina, Atlanta, and Tennessee. The demand for what we had had me feeling like Frank Lucas, but I was determined to stay far enough away from the dope that no one would know it was me. Sophia had done a good job insulating herself too, and anyone we hired went through the most aggressive background check Brewer could come up with. Not only that, but anyone fucking with us had to put up collateral, and we only accepted the life of the person they loved the most. There were no foolproof plans in any facet of the hustle, but there was always a way to minimize your risk.

"You already got people in mind to run the spots?" I asked.

She pulled out a piece of paper and I exchanged for the blunt in my hand. I was only familiar with one name, but I'd know who everyone was soon enough.

"I gotta meet up with the detective after school so I'll pass this along. How much dope you got left?"

"Maybe two and a half bricks, and about seventy thousand in the safe," she replied around a cloud of smoke.

"You gonna be able to move all the product by next week?"

"I don't see why we gotta rush it. I mean, he already got his return and it was early," she replied logically.

"True, but he never told me that paying him early made my timetable flexible."

"Then maybe you should ask him. We got some good shit and we're making money, but moving fast could put us on the wrong people's radar."

I knew she wasn't only taking about the feds, but the jack boys as well. Knowing who they were was just another perk of dealing with Brewer, but that didn't necessarily stop them from making a move against us. There were niggas with their noses in the air and their ears to the street, so it was always smart to move with caution.

"You're right, I'll holla at him. Did you check on that other thing for me?" I asked.

"I went to the address you gave me and it's an inpatient rehab center, but I didn't see your mom. I can try to kick a few dollars at somebody on the inside and find out how she's doing if you want."

"Nah, I'ma do like she asked and let her do this for herself. I just wish she would call more. It's been a whole week since I talked to her."

"You think she knows what you're into?" Sophia asked, passing me the blunt back.

I contemplated that question while puffing slowly and retracing my steps over the past few weeks. I knew my mother wasn't stupid, which was part of the reason I'd been making sure that my ass was in school, because that would've caught her attention. I'd done my best to keep everything normal, but she'd asked me on more than one occasion what the deal was with Lilliana and me because she hadn't been around. I had no answer for that question, especially since Lilliana had been radio silent with me. I missed her, but I was getting money all day, and still fucking Sophia damn near every night. I was winning!

"I don't think she knows anything except that Lilliana and I ain't been kicking it."

"She still ain't talking to you?" she asked.

"You almost sound concerned, but we both know that ain't true."

"Concerned? No, but I don't want to be your choice by default," she replied honestly.

"I don't even know how you could say some shit like that when I literally chose you over her."

"I just wanted to hear you say that," she replied, smiling from ear to ear before leaning over to kiss me tenderly.

We both knew that I still had love for Lilliana, but what Sophia and I had was growing steadily. If Lilliana wasn't careful, she'd lose her spot.

"Don't start nothing I can't finish. You know I gotta get back to class," I said, sliding my free hand under her wife beater and pinching her braless nipple.

"Don't *you* start nothing you can't finish. I do need to run something past you before you go though."

"Okay," I replied slowly, noticing that her tone had gone from playfully sexy to serious.

"It's time for me to move to a new place, nothing too fancy or flashy, but something bigger than a shoebox."

"Okay," I said again, prompting her to continue when she fell silent.

When she sat back in the driver's seat of her car, causing my hand to slip from her titty, I didn't know what to think.

"I was just wondering if you would come check out a couple spots with me. Maybe give me your opinion."

"I *know* that's not what has you acting weird right now. Girl, you know I'll do that," I replied, laughing.

"Cool. And maybe I'll get a spot big enough for you to leave some stuff over if you want."

When I looked her in the eyes, I saw that the statement she'd just made was what had her nervous. She wasn't asking me to find *her* an apartment; she wanted to find *us* an apartment.

"You sure?" I asked.

"I think so, yeah, but I mean, if you don't think - "

"I think we'll figure something out," I said, putting the blunt in the ashtray so that I could pull her towards me and kiss her thoroughly.

It was a full five minutes before we came up for air, and I knew if I didn't get out of the car, we were gonna have to test the shocks one time.

"How about this weekend?" she asked.

"All you gotta do is say the word."

"Okay. Are you coming over after you meet up with your guy?" she asked, visibly more relaxed.

"Of course. So go handle the business because I'm trying to kick back and watch a movie or something."

"I'll settle for 'or something'," she replied seductively.

"I bet you will," I said, dropping a quick kiss on her lips before opening the passenger's door and stepping out.

After flashing her a quick smile, I shut the door and made my way back to the school, noticing that the outside picnic tables were empty, which signaled lunch being over. I still managed to make it to my chemistry class on time, but the lime green we'd smoked had my brain foggy. I somehow made it through my last three periods on auto pilot, and thankfully by the time I met Brewer at Burger King, I was sober again. The look on his face told me that I definitely needed to be.

"We've got a problem," he said as soon as I slid into the booth across from him.

"Sounds serious."

"Every problem is serious, Maxwell, especially the ones we don't anticipate. It's common courtesy that law enforcement of any kind let the locals know when they're going to be operating within their jurisdiction. This morning I was notified that the DEA received a tip about a major drug operation taking place right here in Fayetteville. You wanna guess whose name came up?" he asked ominously.

I already had a sinking feeling in the pit of my stomach, and I didn't really need to hear my name because I wouldn't be sitting across from him for any other reason.

"How close are they looking at me?"

"Oh, it's not you they're looking at, but I'm sure that you're acquainted with Sophia Dettger," he replied.

"Sophia? How the fuck did they get *her* name?"

"That's where it gets interesting. They've got a confidential informant, and they probably wouldn't have disclosed her identity if they didn't need eyes on her until they get to town. Their C.I is Lilliana," he said, looking me dead in the eyes to make sure that I understood how serious he was.

"There's no way," I whispered in disbelief.

He didn't say anything to try to convince me that he was telling the truth. He simply let his statement hang between us. I couldn't believe that my Lilliana would stoop so low as to try and get Sophia locked up. She wasn't that type of petty bitch. I didn't have a verbal argument to give Brewer though, and sticking up for her could come back to haunt me if he was telling the truth.

"Hypothetically speaking, if Lilliana did that she would need more than just her word to make the feds investigate, right?" I asked.

"Ordinarily I'd say yeah, but unfortunately for us, her statement aligns itself with a recent rise in heroin overdoses. That means at the very least, the feds want to take a look around down here."

"Is there anything that you can do to stop that from happening?" I asked, becoming more distressed.

"You already know the answer to that question."

He was right, I did know the answer to that question, because if he interceded, it would draw attention to him, and we couldn't have that.

"I need to talk to her and find out what the fuck is going on," I said.

"I figured you'd feel that way. Come on, let's take a ride," he replied, sliding out of the booth.

I followed his lead, still trying to process what the fuck was going down, but my mind was spinning in circles. Lilliana had never struck me as the type of chick who could or would snitch! I mean, she was square in a lot of ways, but I hadn't seen this move as one she would make. How else could it be explained though? It didn't matter how justified she felt because the results of her actions would be the same. She could've cost me my life.

"You want me to follow you?" I asked.

"Nah, we'll come back for your car."

I hopped in the passenger seat of his forest green Expedition and we got on the move. I didn't bother asking where we were going because I figured that he would tell me if he wanted me to know. Instead, I used the time to try and figure out how I was gonna handle the mess that Lilliana had made for me. I knew that I needed to let Sophia know what was going on, but talking on the phone seemed like a bad idea right now.

"Is this gonna take long? Because I need to let Sophia know what's up face to face," I said.

"Nah, it won't take long."

Twenty minutes later we pulled up at a rundown house in the rural area outside the city.

"Come on," he instructed, climbing out of the truck.

I hesitated for a moment as the thought of these being my last moments popped into my head. I was only able to shake that feeling using the logical reasoning that if Brewer planned to kill me, he wouldn't have been the last person to be seen in public with me. I got out and followed him up the broken, rotted out steps and through the door that was barely hanging on its hinges. The smell of many different animals, dead and alive, spoke to the fact that no one had lived here in a while. In case that wasn't enough though, the fact that the floor looked like a landfill was a clear indication that no one in their right mind lived here.

"What are we doing?" I asked, carefully stepping around and over piles of trash that had the potential to move.

"You'll see."

Again it crossed my mind that this could be that long kiss goodnight, but I followed on as he rounded a corner and began descending some stairs. For a moment I couldn't see where we were going because it was pitch black at the bottom, but suddenly the beam from his flashlight illuminated our path. I could see that the stairs led into an unfinished basement, but before I got to the bottom, I heard the sound of muffled screams, and that filled me with dread. Even before he shinned the light on her naked body strapped to a chair in the middle of the floor, I knew what I would see. The terror in her eyes was evident, but when he shifted the light so she could see me, I saw unspeakable relief come over her.

"You ain't gotta do her like that, man, we don't even know if - "

"If you would stop talking, you'd learn more, young nigga. Lilliana, I want you to tell Maxwell the truth," Brewer said, pulling the gag out of her mouth.

"Max, I'm s-sorry! Please, tell him to let me go," she begged, tears streaming steadily down her face.

"I didn't say beg or apologize. I said tell him the truth about what you did," Brewer stated calmly.

"I-I tipped off the Feds about Sophia," she admitted tear-fully.

"But why, babe? Why would you do some shit like that?" I asked, devastated by her revelation.

"I wanted her out of our lives, out of *your* life. I wanted things to go back to how they used to be when it was just us," she replied.

"But getting her knocked could've cost me my life or my freedom too, don't you see that?" I asked, fighting against the wave of emotions that I was feeling.

My question was met with silence, but I thought I saw something like regret in her eyes. I also thought I saw an ugly truth too.

"You didn't care if I got caught, huh?" I asked, playing my hunch.

"Of course I care. I didn't want you to go to jail, but I thought if that bitch did, then you would get out of the streets," she replied.

Her logic was as sound as it was treacherous, and I couldn't trust someone who would try to manipulate me like that.

"I can't fuck with you no more," I declared.

The sound of a round being chambered into a pistol echoed off of the musty basement walls, and out of the darkness came a gun for me to take.

"What am I supposed to do with this?" I asked, trying to misunderstand that.

"M-Max you can't do it. You love me and I know you love me. Besides, I'm carrying your baby," Lilliana said, distress lacing her words.

"My baby?" I asked, shocked by her revelation.

"Yes, I'm pregnant. Now untie me from this chair and take me home."

I was hearing her words, but my eyes were locked on Brewer because I was trying to decipher what he was thinking. I didn't see any compassion in his eyes. In fact, all I saw was a question, the question he'd asked me not so long ago. Could I admit that I wanted this life and everything that came with it? I'd admitted it then, and said that I would do what was necessary to play this game the right way. Now I was being tested.

"Study long, you study wrong," Brewer said, still extending the gun towards me.

I tool it with reluctance and a heavy heart.

"Max, the baby - "

Those were Lilliana's last words before I fired two shots into her brain, rendering her forever silent.

"I'll take care of the clean up later. You want me to get rid of the gun for you?" he asked calmly, like we were discussing less trivial shit than cold-blooded murder.

"My body, my gun," I replied, tucking it into the waist of my jeans.

"Fine by me. Let's go."

The walk back to his truck was the longest of my life, but the ride back to my car seemed even longer. I knew what I'd done, but I couldn't *believe* what I'd done. Looking back on it in my mind's eye I couldn't see me pulling the trigger. I saw somebody else. A stranger.

"Tell your girl to lay low until the heat blows over. I'll have some other business ventures for you by the end of the week," he said.

I didn't respond. I simply got out of his truck and climbed behind the wheel of my car. I drove around aimlessly for about an hour before finally going to Sophia's house. I had no idea how to tell her what had just happened, but I knew I had to. I'd barely knocked on the door before she snatched it open, and I could tell by her expression that something was wrong.

"I been calling you for hours. Why didn't you answer?" she demanded.

"It's a long story, but I - "

"Fuck it, we gotta go," she said, pulling the door closed.

"Go where?"

"The hospital. It's your mom."

Chapter 10

"Are you gonna tell me what the fuck is going on?" I asked once we were in my car and I'd left a cloud of smoke behind us.

"Look, I knew you were worried about your mom so I went back to the rehab spot with the intentions of paying for information. What I found out was that your mom ain't been there in a week, which probably explains why she didn't call you. I kicked a few more dollars so that anyone who seen her would call me because I knew you'd want to know where she was. I got the call a couple hours ago that she was in the hospital from an overdose."

"How the fuck do you overdose on crack? The goddamn high don't even last that long," I said angrily, shaking my head.

"It wasn't crack."

"What do you mean it wasn't crack? That's my mom's drug of choice," I replied, confused.

"That may have been in the past, but she overdosed on heroin this time."

"Ain't no way," I said, shaking my head again.

When I looked over at Sophia I could tell that she wanted to be lying to me, and she even hoped she was wrong, but she was giving me the information that was given to her. There was nothing I could say without having all the facts, so we rode on in silence.

"Do you wanna tell me what happened at your meeting?" she asked a few minutes later.

"No," I replied simply.

Thankfully she didn't push it because I was literally on emotional overload right now. It took ten minutes for me to get to the hospital, but once I did, I just sat in the car.

"We going in?" Sophia asked.

"I don't know. I mean what am I supposed to say to her? If she overdosed on heroin, then she overdosed on a product that I put in the street. So I guess shooting her wasn't enough for me," I replied bitterly.

"I know why you're trying to blame yourself, but you can't make your mother's decisions for her. She's grown. Right now what's important is being there for her, so let's go."

I couldn't admit that Sophia was right, but I did open my door and get out with her. We walked into the emergency room hand in hand, and I was headed for the front desk when I saw a familiar face.

"Megan, can you tell me what room my mom is in?" I asked.

I could tell that she recognized me from when my mom had been admitted with a gunshot wound, but she also had a strange look on her face.

"Uh, let me check," she replied, moving behind the desk and speaking to another nurse.

"No matter what happens, don't get mad at your mom," Sophia warned.

"I just don't understand her fucking with heroin. That's not how she gets down."

"If I was guessing, I'd say it was a result of the pain medicine they had her on in the hospital. I bet they gave her a morphine drip right after surgery, then Percocet's when she was discharged. A lot of people move to heroin from pills, and you know what they say about heroin. You try it once and you're hooked from there on," Sophia replied.

I couldn't fault her logic, but that didn't make it any easier to deal with the role I'd played in all of this. Her needing pain medication was my fault, but I kept this comment to myself because I didn't want Sophia trying to cheer me up. I had to live with what I'd done.

"I can smell what you're thinking, Maxwell, and you need to stop it. If you're guilty, what does that make me?" she asked.

The words that I was gonna speak were not the ones she wanted to hear, but thankfully, Megan's approach forced me to chew on them.

"Your mom's doctor is coming to talk to you," Megan said.

"I can talk to whoever that is after I see my mom. What room is she in?" I asked.

"If you'll just wait for the doctor, he'll be with you in a few minutes," Megan insisted.

"Listen, I understand what you're saying, but whatever the doctor has to say ain't more important than me seeing my mom first, so - "

My sentence was interrupted by Sophia grabbing my arm, but when I looked at her she was staring at Megan with a haunted expression on her face.

"What's wrong with you?" I asked, looking at her and then at Megan.

It wasn't until they both looked at me that I felt a chill that I would never forget.

"No. Don't look at me like that because if my mom were dead I would *know* it," I said forcefully.

"I'm so sorry, Mr. Cooper."

"No, no. No! Don't lie to me!" I yelled, lunging forward and grabbing Megan by the throat.

"Max, stop! Stop it!" Sophia yelled, trying to pull me away from the now-struggling nurse.

"She's lying," I growled through clenched teeth while steadily applying pressure.

"No she's not, baby. Your mom is gone."

The softness with which Sophia had spoken those words pierced the fog in my brain, forcing me to let the nurse go. I turned around to find Sophia staring at me with eyes full of the guilt I felt and tears that mirrored the saltiness I could taste in my mouth. I didn't need her to repeat what she'd said, nor did I need anyone to confirm it. I said that I would know if my mother was dead, and I did, so there was nothing left to say.

Sophia opened her arms to me, but I moved past her and headed for the front entrance. I could hear her calling my name, but I didn't stop or look back, I simply kept moving forward so that I didn't collapse under the weight of my guilt. I managed to make it to my car, throw myself behind the wheel, and speed off before I started sobbing uncontrollably. I only made it a block down the road before I had to pull over so that I could throw up violently. Once I managed to get that under control I jumped back on the road, weaving in and out of traffic, running red lights and stop signs without giving a fuck who got hurt because of me. I had no thought for the direction I was headed, but I somehow arrived at my apartment twenty minutes later. It took me another ten minutes to work up the nerve to go inside, and when I did, all I was able to do was curl up in my mom's bed and cry. I cried for hours, until there were no more tears left and exhaustion finally took over, and then I slept.

When I finally woke up it was two a.m., but I knew what I had to do. I packed a bag of clothes, grabbed a couple guns and my money, left my cell phone on the table, and I left my apartment for the last time. The memories there were too painful to live with, just like the memory of Fayetteville as a whole. In order to survive, I would have to start over. I'd heard before that you could never truly outrun your past, and I was about to put that theory to the test. I didn't know where I was going. I just knew I couldn't wait to get there.

ASAD

Chapter 11
10 years later 2018
Las Vegas, NV

"Max? Max, wake up, baby, it's okay."

The soothing sound of her voice somehow penetrated the fog that had me lost in my nightmare, and I was finally able to wake up. I could feel my heart hammering in my chest and the sweat pouring from my body into the sheets, but I was awake, and that's what I focused on. In my nightmare I'd been strapped to a table while my mother stuck needle after needle full of heroin into all the veins in my body. Right before she pushed the poison into my system, she told me that she loved me. I'd had the same dream over and over for the last ten years, sometimes once a month, and other times it came every night for a week straight. I never actually saw myself die, but I knew that there was no way to survive an injection like that of ninety-seven percent pure heroin. I knew that painful truth all too well.

"I'm good," I said, extracting myself from Deliah's embrace and climbing out of bed to head for the shower.

Deliah had been in my life for the last two years so she was used to these episodes, but I still felt embarrassed by them, especially when we had company. The sour smell of my own sweat made me want to throw up, but I managed to step into the shower and turn the hot water up as high as it would go before that happened. The immediate pain shocked my senses enough to fully release me from the demons that haunted me at night and after five minutes, I was able to lower the water temperature to a normal level.

As I expected, the shower door opened and Deliah's naked body waded into the steam with me. This was our routine, which is why it did surprise me that she didn't come alone this time. Deliah was gorgeous. She stood 5'10", weighed a curvy 160 pounds, had flawless skin the color of ginger snap cookies, and had eyes that I called hazel honey sunshine. She was more than enough woman for me, but we both had healthy sexual appetites that required a snack even after a five course meal. Thankfully we never had to look far. Trailing behind Deliah was last night's snack, an equally beautiful 5'2", 140 pound Mexicana named Lupe, who was thicker than a bread truck and not bashful in the slightest. Proof of her boldness came in the way she closed the shower door behind them and immediately dropped to her knees in front of me. Before I could open my mouth she had hers working overtime, slurping my dick up like it was what she needed to live.

"I figured that you'd need to decompress more than usual. It seemed worse than a normal nightmare," Deliah said softly, moving behind me so she could wash my back the way I liked.

"I appreciate your consideration," I replied genuinely, wrapping my left hand up in Lupe's long black hair and pulling her towards me faster.

With each passing second the bad memories faded and I became lost in the moment.

"She's good, right?" Deliah whispered into my ear before lightly grazing my lobe with her teeth.

"Uh huh," I moaned.

"Let's see what she can do on her own," Deliah suggested.

I reluctantly released my grip on her hair, but I quickly discovered that I wasn't mad about it. With one hand wrapped firmly around my dick, she moved her mouth to my balls and began sucking them while jacking me off vigorously. I looked down to find her dark brown eyes blazing with desire back up at me, and that only turned me on more.

"Fuck," I moaned, fighting not to cum yet.

"Enjoy it, baby," Deliah said, wrapping her arms around my upper body, pressing her warm, wet flesh against mine.

It was like Lupe knew my body because right before my climax reached the point of no return, she popped my dick back in between her succulent lips and drank me until there was nothing left except my trembling. I thought that would be the end of it, but I was wrong. Lupe grabbed me by my ass cheeks and forced my dick down her throat until I thought she would choke, but she didn't. What she did was use her throat and mouth like jumper cables, bringing my dick back to life within minutes.

"Baby, baby, I - "

"I told you she was good," Deliah said, moving from behind me to stand next to Lupe.

Once I was rock hard again, Lupe took deep throating to the next level, putting her hands behind her back while devouring me slowly. As phenomenal as her technique was, it was the look of pure pleasure in her eyes that turned me on the most and had me wanting to give it all back. When I looked at Deliah, I saw that she was enjoying this almost as much as I was, but that didn't surprise me because she liked to watch.

"Come here," I demanded, extending my hand towards her.

"Hold on a second," she said, tapping Lupe on the shoulder.

Lupe pulled back long enough for me to grab Deliah around the waist and toss her into the air. Deliah's hands clenched the solid steel bar that ran the length of the shower and her legs found their way around my neck. My hands immediately went to her juicy ass cheeks, pulling her pussy to me so the feast could begin.

"Mmm, th-that's it, baby," Deliah moaned passionately.

Lupe took that as her cue and got back to trying to sucking the skin off of my dick. We were officially a three ring circus, and everybody was in love with the show. I managed to make Deliah cum twice before Lupe had my knees too weak to concentrate. With Deliah satisfied, I put her down and I turned my sights on Lupe. Picking her up, I slip deep inside her already throbbing pussy and pinned her to the wall with pounding blows that had her speaking incoherent Spanish rapidly.

"Don't cum in her," Deliah said.

"Just be ready," I replied, fucking Lupe harder.

It was only minutes later when Lupe screamed her way to orgasm, and I had to pull out of her because her pussy was making it impossible for me not to cum. I put Lupe down and turned to find Deliah bent over and ready for me. I quickly pushed my way inside her tight pussy hard enough to run her into the wall, but not even that would stop me, forcing me to lean against the shower wall for support.

"B-bathe him," Deliah instructed Lupe while fighting to catch her breath.

Without hesitation she grabbed the soap and washcloth and thoroughly did just that. Once she was done Deliah dismissed her and we stayed under the water's pounding spray together.

"How do you feel?" Deliah asked, searching my face intently.

I knew she wasn't asking about my physical well-being, especially after what had just happened, so I wasn't about to play coy.

"You know I always gets sad around the anniversary date."

"You called out her name," Deliah said.

"Did I? Well, my mom was - "

"Not your mom's name. Sophia's," she said, putting her hand gently on my cheek.

I knew that my expression was out of shock because I hadn't thought about Sophia, much less mentioned her name, in a long time. Over the years I'd told Deliah almost everything about my past, including the girl I'd left behind without a backwards glance. At first I'd thought that I'd left Sophia to avoid killing her because I considered her partially responsible for my mom's overdose. It took me awhile to own the full weight of what happened, but with that came the realization that I'd left Sophia because I loved her, but couldn't be with her. There would've been no way for me to look at her and not see death. Lilliana's death, my mom's death, and ultimately Detective Brewer's death because I'd made the trip back to conclude that part of my life four years ago. I had no idea why I'd called out Sophia's name, but she was definitely not a conscious thought for me anymore.

"You know like I do that that's beyond weird," I replied.

"I do know that, and that's why I'm concerned."

"I appreciate that, babe, but you took my mind off of everything that happened, and I'm good," I said, leaning down to kiss her thoroughly.

There were two things that we'd always reserved for each other, and that was the fact that I wouldn't cum in another female, and we only kissed each other. We may have invited women into our bed, but we kept the intimacy between us.

"So, what do you have planned for today?" she asked, wrapping her arms around my neck and bringing us body to body.

"Petty and I gotta put our move down on Big Bernard and his operation."

"Is this off the books?" she asked.

"Until it's on the books."

Like anybody else, my past had lit the path for my future, and that was why I'd joined the police academy six years ago. Brewer had given me the blueprint, but after making detective last year in the narcotics division, my partner Tyreek Pettybone and I changed the game. Petty was a street nigga just like me, which meant we had no love for the law, but we were down to use it to our advantage. So we went after big dope boys and took everything of value, including their lives, before turning their organizations over and shutting them down from good. It was a dirty job, and we were the perfect somebodies to do it.

"Will you be out late?" she asked.

"I don't know, why?"

"I've got a couple new girls coming over, and I thought you might want to help with the interview process," she replied, smiling in that naughty way that excited me.

Deliah was owner and operator of her own whore house, Dream Catchers, and even with selling pussy being legal in Nevada, she still killed the competition because her girls were second to none. As the man in her life, she always offered me the first ride when it came to new or perspective talent, as long as she was riding shotgun.

"I'll beat the sun home, but that's about all I can guarantee, sweetheart," I said.

"That's always been good enough for me."

This time when we kissed, I knew what it was leading to. It was another pleasurable twenty minutes before we stumbled out of the shower and made our way back to the bedroom.

Deliah had a spacious two story ranch house just outside the city limits, and only a select handful of girls were allowed to live with her here instead of at the other house she kept for business. One of the few rules Deliah had was that no one entered her bedroom without permission, so when we came into the room to find four women waiting inside with the door closed, we knew something was wrong. Deliah immediately stepped in front of me to shield my naked body from view. Her movement was unconscious, but it spoke to how she really felt about me, especially given the fact that I'd fucked two out of the four already.

"What's wrong?" Deliah asked.

A short brunette named Cassandra stepped forward, obviously the decided spokesperson for whatever this was.

"It's Jessica and Amber. No one has seen or heard from them since that private party they flew to Fresno for yesterday," Cassandra said.

"They missed their check-in times?" Deliah asked.

"Yes, and that's not like them, but we figured that they were busy keeping the client happy since he'd flown them out there especially," Cassandra replied.

Deliah's girls were all like sisters and they stayed in touch on a regular basis because that's how Deliah wanted it. Everybody had to know where everybody was because they were their sister's keeper.

"Have there been any posts on Facebook or any social media site?" Deliah asked.

"No," Cassandra replied anxiously.

When Deliah turned around to face me I could see the worry in her eyes, and I knew what she needed.

"I'll take care of it. You and the girls stay by the phone."

ASAD

Chapter 12

"What's good, Bigman?" I asked, pulling up alongside Petty's 2018 Dodge Charger in a pawnshop parking lot off of the strip.

"Shit, waiting on your slow ass. What took you so long anyway?"

The smile I couldn't keep off of my face made him screw his face up in mock disgust. We both knew it was jealousy though because he'd give his left nut for a situation like I had with Deliah, even though he loved his wife.

"I hope you ate a good breakfast when you were down because we've got a long day ahead of us," he stated.

"Well, I definitely ate *something*, but I don't know if it's the nutritional breakfast you're talking about."

"And they call *me* Petty," he replied, shaking his head, causing me to laugh.

"You know I would invite you over, but I know Ayana will bust that pistol, and I'm not about to have your angry black woman on my ass. Especially because that'll have *my* angry black woman on my ass!" I said truthfully.

"Facts. Dig it though, I did like you asked and reached out to Fresno vice squad about your people. If shit ain't right we'll be the first call that they make."

"I appreciate that, bruh. You know all of Deliah's girls are family to her and they wouldn't worry unnecessarily," I replied.

"I was surprised when you texted me about it because Deliah runs a tight operation and her ladies toe the line better than any other stable I've seen out here."

"Facts. So when are we gonna make the move on De boy?" I asked, shifting the focus to today's business.

"The move is made. I was just waiting on you," he replied, smiling.

I knew that smile, and it indicated that he was on his bull-shit.

"What you mean the move is made, my nigga?"

"So you think I'm just big for nothing, huh? Like my 6'4", 250 pounds don't weigh in because that nigga Bernard is 6'7" and 300 pounds? Come on, bruh, I knocked that nigga out with a nice three piece, I mean straight snoozed him," Petty declared, laughing.

"Bullshit!"

"When you ever known me to lie about a fight?" he asked seriously.

We both knew the answer to that question, and I'd seen him handle plenty of motherfuckers rough when it came to shooting a fade.

"So where is he?" I asked.

"In the trunk, where else?"

"You really riding around with a nigga in the trunk at ten a.m.?" I asked, no longer seeing the humor in the situation.

"Who the fuck is gonna pull *me* over?"

He had a point. Despite us both driving unmarked Chargers, it was still obvious that they were cop cars, so nobody was gonna do a routine traffic stop.

"A'ight, so let's go handle that situation and get it out of the way first," I suggested.

"That's cool. I already talked to our guy over at that new scuba shop and he's got what we need."

"I'll follow you," I said, pulling off to make a quick U-turn.

There wasn't a lot of people that I trusted, but Petty was one of them. We came from similar poverty-stricken backgrounds, and we'd had the same determination to make it out at all costs. From day one in the police academy we'd been as thick as thieves, and once we became partners, that bond only grew stronger. When we became partners in crime, it was like finding the brother that I always wanted. It was a different type of hustle when it was a nigga that had your back because the emotional landmines that existed with females was non-existent. We got to the money, no more, no less.

As I followed him out of the parking lot I sent Deliah a text letting her know that we'd contacted the cops in Cali, and now all we could do was wait. I knew that wouldn't be easy for her, but unless she wanted me to take a road trip or hop a flight, there was nothing more that I could do. Right now my focus needed to be on the task at hand, but if I was being real with myself, part of what happened in the shower earlier was still on my mind. The part where Deliah said I called out Sophia's name. The moments when I'd thought about her in the last decade had been fleeting. The last time had actually been when I'd journeyed back to Fayetteville to pay Brewer a visit. I'd wondered if she was still around, but I hadn't seen what good would come from trying to find the answer to that question. So I'd slipped in under the cover of night and caught Brewer sleeping, literally. Strangely enough, he understood why he had to die and he didn't beg for his life, so with two headshots I'd thought I'd forever closed that chapter of my life. For some reason I felt like even thinking about Sophia was history's attempt at a rewrite, and I wasn't having it.

Thankfully my mind centered back on more pressing business as we pulled into the parking lot of the scuba shop. I had no idea what would make a motherfucker open a scuba shop in the desert, but Las Vegas was a place that embraced the weird shit. I sat in my car while Petty ran inside, and five minutes later he came out carrying what we needed. Once he deposited it onto his backseat, he came to my driver side window.

"The spot I picked is about thirty minutes away, and it's your turn to dig the hole," he informed me.

"I got my shovel, nigga, but I need to get some food first so I'ma hit that McDonalds drive-thru real quick."

"Only you would eat before a move like this," he replied, shaking his head and going back to his car.

"Damn right, I'm hungry as fuck!" I admitted.

Thankfully there was no line and I was able to get my Big Mac in four minutes. I made sure to multitask and eat while I was driving so that by the time we got out to the wide open desert a half an hour, later I was ready to work. I pulled up right next to Petty, got out, and got my shovel out of the trunk. By the time I made it back to the front of my car, Petty had the trunk of his car open and he was pulling a barely conscious Bernard out.

"Damn, how hard did you hit him?" I asked.

"Just a few love taps, ain't that right, Bernard?" he asked, dropping him face first on the hard sand.

"F-fuck you, bitch," Bernard mumbled angrily.

His comment earned him a swift kick to the stomach that had him whaling sand like a mummy movie. I decided to let them have their fun while I started digging a hole about a foot away. Days like this were why I'd maintained my workout regimen and athletic build even after I'd quit high school to pursue my G.E.D. This wasn't the first hole I'd dug, and I knew that it took patience as much as strength, so I set a steady rhythm and zoned out. Most people started asking questions within the first fifteen minutes of me digging, but Bernard lasted an entire hour before inquiring about what the hole was for. Of course I was too busy to answer, and all my partner did was laugh like the petty motherfucker that he was. It took two full hours to get the hole dug to its necessary depth, and by then I was gassed, but the work was only beginning.

"Showtime," I said, joining Petty next to a sick-looking Bernard.

"Okay, Bernard, here's the deal. We know who you are and what you do, and the good run you had has now reached its conclusion. That's unfortunate for you, but fortunate for us because you're gonna give up all the info on your operation, including the money you've stashed," Petty said.

"Let me guess: if I don't cooperate, you're gonna put me in that hole," he replied sarcastically.

"No, that hole ain't for you. It's for Raymonique," I replied calmly.

The change in his demeanor was instantaneous at the mention of his nineteen-year-old daughter, and I doubted that there would be any more sarcastic commentary.

"Look, she ain't got nothing to do with - "

"She doesn't, but she'll have *everything* to do with it if you force our hands," Petty said.

"We want your connect, your workers, the stash houses, the whole nine yards. And the money too, like my partner said," I reiterated.

"You know I can't do that! You trying to get my whole fucking family killed, you crooked piece of shit!" Bernard yelled angrily.

"No harm will come to your family because no one will know that you told us. It's not like you'll be called into court to testify," Petty assured him.

"So I'm supposed to believe that if I give you what you want, you'll just let me go?" Bernard asked, skeptically.

"Why would you believe that? Nah, you're *definitely* gonna die my nigga. The only question that remains unanswered is, are you going alone, or is your daughter going too?" I said seriously.

"Y-you're a cop, you can't - "

His sentence was interrupted by me and Petty immediately laughing at his appeal to our good nature.

"You *can't* be serious. Is that really the argument that you're gonna try to make, you're gonna appeal to our civic duty?" I asked.

"Man, shut that shit up or I'ma bring your daughter out here and let you watch while niggas run a train on her, and *then* I'ma blow her fucking head off," Petty threatened.

"A'ight look, I'll give up the money I got, but I can't give you the rest."

"He still think we playing, huh?" I asked.

"Guess so. I'll be back shortly," Petty replied, closing his trunk before getting in his car and leaving.

"W-where's he going?" Bernard asked.

I ignored the question, got back into my own car, and relaxed under the air conditioning. I killed time by texting back and forth with Deliah, trying to keep her calm because she was beyond worried now. Not only had she not heard from Jessica and Amber, but the clients who'd contracted them weren't answering either. I couldn't downplay her fears because I had a bad feeling now too, but I was hoping that I was wrong. Despite Deliah and I being in an open, honest relationship I tried not to interfere with her business too much. We didn't have secrets necessarily because she'd always answer any question I had, but the one I was about to ask pushed the limits. Surprisingly enough, she shot me all the client's info within minutes, and I used the next hour to call in favors from here to Cali. I still hadn't heard anything when Petty pulled back up beside me forty-five minutes later, but I planned to give it my undivided attention once we were finished up here.

"Everything straight?" I asked, getting out of my car.

"Yep," Petty replied, again going to his trunk.

This time when he opened it he reached in and pulled out a blindfolded, slender-built, brown skin chick, and he tossed her to the ground just as roughly.

"Mother-*fucker!*" Bernard exclaimed, trying his best to get his feet under him so that he could stand up.

"You couldn't beat my nigga when your hands were free, so stop acting like if you get up you've got a chance now," I said, kicking the wind out of him with a well-placed boot to the chest.

"A'ight, nigga, you know we ain't bullshitting, so what are we gonna do?" Petty asked.

"Dad, *please*, give them whatever they want," Ray-monique whined.

"Y'all got it, I'll tell you everything. Just d-don't hurt her," Bernard replied defeatedly.

"Finally, the nigga gets some act right," I said, pulling out my phone so I could record his words.

"I got this, bruh, get everything ready," I said, nodding towards his backseat.

While Petty got down to one last detail I stepped closer to Bernard so he could speak into the mic.

"Start talking, nigga," I demanded.

I could see the hate in his eyes, but I had no mercy for him or anyone else selling drugs. My purpose wasn't to protect and serve motherfuckers like him. It was to dismantle and eradicate them from the face of the Earth. Even if that meant that I had to do it one body at a time. It took big bad Bernard fifteen minutes to spill his guts about the operation he was overseeing for his Cali connect. He gave up the stash houses, workers, location of his hard drugs with crypto currently on them, even the drop spots between here and Los Angeles.

"You do understand that all of this will have to be verified, right?" I asked once he was done talking.

"Do what the fuck you gotta do, just let my daughter go," he replied.

"I don't work like that exactly," Petty said, pulling the girl to her feet.

"I just told you motherfuckers everything I know, now let my daughter go!" he demanded angrily.

In response, Petty pulled a standard issue Glock .40 from his waist and smacked Raymonique viciously over the head with it, rendering her unconscious. She folded nice and quiet like soft linen, but Bernard howled like it was a full moon and he was in real pain. When Petty tossed me the gun so that he could slip the oxygen mask over Raymonique's head, I caught it and immediately jammed it in the big man's mouth.

"Are you *sure* you told us everything, and gave us the right information? Nod real slow if you're sure," I said patiently.

He complied without hesitation.

"Good. So if your info is real, then you've got nothing to worry about. She's got enough air to breathe underground for a few hours at least," I assured him.

Of course this comment had him trying to act a fool again, which was wearing on what little patience I had left, so I did the only thing left for me to do. I pulled the trigger twice.

"Damn, I thought he would *never* shut the fuck up," Petty said, carrying Raymonique to the hole I'd dug and laying her down on it.

"Right. You got this while I go pick up the money?" I asked, tucking the pistol in the waist of my pants.

"Oh, so now I gotta dig a hole for that big bastard *and* cover her up?"

"I'll take care of the next one all by myself," I vowed, already moving towards my car.

"Yeah, I've heard that before. You might as well verify everything else while you're at it, do some recon on the locations he gave up, and then we'll meet up at the station."

"How long she got?" I asked.

"Three and a half hours."

"A'ight, I'll call you," I said, climbing behind the wheel and pulling off.

My first stop was Bernard's high rise apartment, where I found two different hard drives that he claimed held a total of five million in crypto-currency.

That wasn't a bad day's work, if I said so myself. My plan was to hit his stash houses next because there was probably hard cash scattered throughout those, but as soon as I got back in the car I saw four missed calls from Deliah. I immediately called her back, but for the first few minutes of our call, I couldn't understand shit that she was saying because she was crying so hard. And then I did understand. The Oakland P.D had found two dead bodies, and they were Amber and Jessica.

ASAD

Chapter 13

"Come here," I said, opening my arms wide to Deliah as soon as I came in the house. She immediately ran into my embrace, and the uncontrollable crying that I'd heard on the phone started again.

"I know, bae, I know," I whispered, rubbing her back soothingly.

After a few minutes I could tell that there was no end in sight for the tears she was shedding, so I picked her up and carried her to the bedroom. Sex was the last thing on my mind as I laid her down gently on her bed and crawled in behind her. Instead, I wrapped my arms around her and let her sob until exhaustion forced sleep upon her. My thoughts were scrambled as I listened to her slow breathing and tried to process what would happen next. Death wasn't anything new to me, but what happened to Jessica and Amber hit home and was more personal than the life I'd snuffed out an hour ago. As much as I felt the need to lay with Deliah to comfort and support her, I was also using the quiet surrounding me to deal with the screaming in my brain. It was a full thirty minutes before I slowly unwrapped myself from around Deliah and made my way back into the living room. I wasn't surprised to find ten beautiful women of all shape, colors, and sizes comforting and consoling each other, and all eyes turned on me.

"How's Deliah?" Cassandra asked, coming towards me.

"She's sleeping, and hurting more than I've ever seen, but she'll be okay. How are you all holding up?" I asked, looking around the room.

The glassy eyes full of unshed tears said it all.

"I want to talk to all of you real quick," I said, moving to the middle of the living room.

Everyone gave me their undivided attention and Cassandra stood next to me.

"We're all aware of Deliah's no drug policy, but I know she makes exceptions sometimes. Do any of you think that's what happened?" I asked.

"No. Deliah only makes exceptions for ecstasy or a little molly, but not heroin. She would *never* let us use heroin," Cassandra replied quickly.

"Would Jessica and Amber just disobey the rules like that?" I asked.

Everyone shook their head no, which was what I expected, but I didn't like the conclusion that brought me to.

"Has any of you ever been hired out to that particular client?" I asked.

Again everyone replied with negative shakes of the head.

"I reached out to the girls I know who do private parties, and they hadn't worked with anyone out of Fresno, but one girl has heard about them. They don't know how to take no for an answer," Cassandra said.

"Like raping girls? How the hell would that info not spread to all you girls?" I asked.

"Not rape, just hard partying, and most girls are cool with it because its free drugs on top of what they're already making," Cassandra replied.

I'd had a feeling that Jessica and Amber hadn't been snorting heroin willingly, especially not considering the amount found in their system. They overdosed, but the Oakland P.D. said there was enough blow in their blood to make three NFL linebackers overdose. *Twice*! It wasn't simply the fact that two girls I know had died because of drugs. It was the similarities to my past that had my mind blown. None of these women knew my past, so they probably figured that I was just asking standard police questions. It was more than that though. For years I'd looked for any connection I could find to the killer dope I'd picked up that fateful night in Virginia, but I hadn't come across anything. The purity of the dope found inside Deliah's girls gave me familiar chills, forcing me to admit that the chase for the boogie man of my past was back on.

"Listen, I know you girls probably have appointments and clients lined up, but unless they're a regular their appointment is cancelled until further notice," I said.

"Wh-what about our sisters?" Cassandra asked emotionally.

"As soon as Deliah wakes up I'm leaving for Cali," I said.

"I'm up," Deliah said, coming into the living room.

Immediately all the girls flocked to her and surrounded her with love in the form of hugs and kisses. I could see the immense clouds of sadness floating thru Deliah's eyes, but the strength that she embodied was just as evident. I gave them a moment together before nodding to Deliah to follow me outside, so we could speak in private.

"Thank you," she said, hugging me once we were alone on the porch.

"For what?"

"For everything you've done, and everything you're about to do," she replied.

"You don't have to thank me. I just need to know that you're gonna be okay while I'm gone because I don't know where this journey will lead."

"I'll be fine. I need you to be safe and find out what happened to my girls because they didn't do this to themselves," she insisted.

"I agree. So tell me everything you know about the client."

"They're two brothers, white boys, who own some type of tech company. They embody the motto work hard, play harder, but I've never heard of any serious complaints about how they treat the women they hire. Probably because they double and triple the going rate," she replied.

"I talked to the girls, and Cassandra found out that they party hard by force sometimes. They gotta answer for that now," I vowed, taking her face in my hands.

Staring at her, I saw the love and gratitude she felt towards me, and it was further demonstrated when she surrendered her mouth to my kiss. The taste of her salty tears on my tongue only served to fuel the rage growing inside me, but I fought to keep a lid on that emotion until I could express it thoroughly.

"I'll call you when I'm done making arrangements for the girls to be transported home," I said, pulling back to look at her again.

"Okay. I'm gonna work on giving them a proper burial for them once they arrive."

"I'll try to be back for the service," I replied.

"I'll understand if you're not. I'd rather you be out there personally righting the wrong because we both know that our girls didn't deserve to die like that, or to be thrown away like forgotten trash."

I could see the anger clearly in her eyes and I knew she was thinking about Jessica's and Amber's naked bodies being found in a landfill. She was right, they deserved better.

"Stay strong," I said, kissing her one more time before heading towards my car.

Once I'd slid behind the wheel I texted Petty to find out if he was ready and where he was meeting me. Within moments he was directing me towards the station because he was already there getting approval for us to link up with Oakland P.D. Typically we'd have to let their homicide division handle the case because it was within their jurisdiction, but as soon as I'd found out what happened I'd put the call in to Oakland and let them know that this was personal.

I started my car and got moving in the direction of the precinct while trying to mentally prepare myself for the road that lay ahead. I didn't have to be clairvoyant to know that some people were gonna die, because I wanted answers, and I wouldn't be denied.

When I pulled into the police station parking lot fifteen minutes later, I found Petty waiting for me beside his car. I Carley slowed down long enough for him to hop in before I was racing out of the other entrance to the parking lot.

"What did the captain say?" I asked.

"To make sure none of that heroin hits his street, or we'll both be back on desk duty."

"Who are we looking for from Oakland homicide?" I asked.

"Detectives Marquez and Stevenson, and they're gonna meet us away from the station house so as few people as possible know we're in town. We might have to do some controlled buys," he replied, pulling out his phone.

"Send them a message and tell them that we've been delayed, but we'll be there by morning."

I could feel Petty's eyes on me, looking for an answer to the non-verbal question that he was asking, but I kept my eyes on the road ahead. He eventually took the hint and went about the business of sending the message.

"Okay, it's done. Now do you wanna explain?" he asked a couple minutes later.

"Right now we have info that the Oakland P.D. doesn't have, and even if they did have it, they'd have to pass it off for it to be followed up on. That's too much time that could be wasted, so we're gonna do the leg work, starting with finding out all that we can about Brad Dobs and his brother Chad."

"And who are they?" he asked, already letting his fingers fly over his phone's screen.

"They are the clients who hired Deliah's girls, which means they are the motherfuckers who know what happened. We're gonna be the first ones to ask them about it," I replied, envisioning my hands wrapped around one or both of their throats. One way or another, they were gonna speak the truth.

"Okay, a Google search shows that the Dobs boys own Miratech, which is some type of computer programming company located in Fresno, worth a couple hundred million. They're identical twins, blond hair, green eyes, 6'2", and 190 pounds. No wives, no kids, and they own several estates all around the world. What makes you think they're still in Cali?" he asked.

"Because they think they got away with it by having the bodies dumped away from their base of operations. They're in Fresno, going on with their everyday life because to do anything different would appear suspicious."

"So what's our plan?" he asked, looking over at me.

"You've got three hours to dig as deep as you can and find out everything about these motherfuckers, and then we need to decide where to catch them."

"I'm on it," he replied. Taking our show on the road wasn't an ideal situation, but both of us would go above and beyond to protect those we loved. Or avenge them.

Once I got us on the highway and the miles to our destination grew shorter, I allowed my mind to open to the past I'd been desperate to outrun. The regrets I had about the way I handled my mother's death were numerous, but one of the biggest ones was my delay in looking for answers. My quest to find the manufacture of the poison that had taken my mother's life didn't begin until I'd joined the police force. My excuse had been that I'd lacked the resources to properly investigate, but that was a lie because I'd had money, and there was no better resource when it came to criminal activities. The truth was that I'd been scared to face that particular demon, but had I not been, I might not be traveling this particular road right now. One thing that I knew for sure was that I wouldn't make the same mistakes twice. I *couldn't* do that.

While Petty went to work researching, I began putting together a plan that I hoped would yield the desired results. I called Deliah and told her what I was thinking and how she could help, and I could tell that giving her a task to focus her chaotic emotions on was the best thing I could do. Within two hours, the necessary arrangements had been made. By the time we arrived in downtown Fresno, Pettybone and I had a clear understanding. Somebody was gonna die tonight.

"You sure this gonna work?" Petty asked once we'd pulled into the underground garage at the Four Seasons hotel.

"They already took the bait. Deliah said that she was sending four of her best girls to replace the two that had obviously run off. She sold it like her company's reputation was more valuable than some dead hookers, and they were all too eager to agree with her. The Dobs brothers rented out the penthouse, and Deliah's last text said they're already up there waiting on the girls to arrive."

"How are we getting in?" he asked.

"Service elevator."

"How are we getting them out?" he asked.

In response to this question, I signaled for him to get out of the car and follow me to the trunk. I opened it and grabbed the lone duffle bag I kept stashed in there for emergency purposes.

"We don't gotta bring them out," I said, taking the bag out and closing the trunk.

"What about the cameras?" he asked, following me towards the elevator.

"I called in a favor while you were doing your research."

He didn't ask any more questions after that because we trusted each other with our lives. If he would've asked, I wouldn't have had a problem letting him know that our presence would be erased by the hotel manager himself, because he'd benefitted handsomely from Deliah's business over the years. But he didn't ask, and we rode the elevator to the penthouse in silence. Once we got there, the room door was quickly pulled open after two knocks, but I could tell by how the man's smile vanished that we weren't who he was expecting.

"C-can I help you?"

"Are you Brad or Chad?" I asked.

"I'm Chad, and you are?"

I held up my badge in response and then proceeded to push my way into the hotel suite.

"Wh-what's this about? Don't you need a warrant or something?" Chad asked, clearly two steps away from panicking.

As soon as I saw all the powder scattered across the living room coffee table I understood why.

"So you must be Brad," Petty said, speaking to the man sitting on the couch swiping powder residue off his nose.

"Who the fuck?"

"They're cops, bro," Chad replied immediately.

"You got a warrant?" Brad asked.

I ignored his question while setting my duffle bag on the floor and unzipping it. I could tell by the sudden gasps from both Brad and Chad that the Smith and Wesson 45 I was now screwing a silencer on definitely had their undivided attention.

"Which one of you is older?" I asked, standing up straight with the pistol resting comfortably in my hand.

"I am," Brad said.

I took aim at his face and pulled the trigger twice, splattering his brain matter all over the couch's floral design.

"I guess you're older now, Chad. I hope that makes you smarter."

ASAD

Chapter 14

"Chad? Chad, I'm gonna need you to focus," I said to the now glassy-eyed man staring at what remained of his twin brother.

"Wh-wh-why did you do that?" Chad asked, clearly shaken.

"Because I needed to get your attention so you would answer my questions truthfully. So are you gonna answer my questions, or should I shoot you now?" I asked, aiming the still-smoking pistol at his face.

His lips trembled uncontrollably as he nodded his head in quick jerking motions.

"Good. Now tell me what happened to the two girls you hired out of Vegas a few days ago," I demanded.

"G-girls." He shuddered, guilt filling up the whites of his eyes.

"Yes, girls, Chad. The two girls who overdosed while partying with you," Petty elaborated while moving towards the dope-covered coffee table.

"Th-the partying got a little out of hand, but I don't know exactly what happened."

The bullshit coming out of his mouth was suddenly interrupted by his high screaming. The cause for his screams was the bullet I'd fired through his left kneecap.

"They didn't get to a landfill in Oakland without you knowing, so save the lies or endure a fate worse than death," I promised, squatting down so that I was eye level with the still screaming man.

"I'd take his advice," Petty commented as he started scooping the dope back into the huge Ziploc bag on the table.

"I didn't dump the bodies!" Chad yelled with tears running down his face and mixing with the spit sliding from his mouth.

"Last time I'm gonna ask you nicely, Chad. *What happened?*" I repeated.

"They snorted too much d-dope. We tried to save them, but we couldn't, so we called someone to handle the problem," Chad replied.

"Who did you call?" I asked.

"Our supplier," Chad said quickly.

It was pissing me off having to ask so many questions instead of him volunteering the information that I needed. That forced me to stick the hot silencer on the end of my pistol into his right eye socket, causing him to scream in both pain and panic.

"Motherfucker, tell me *everything*," I growled.

"F-Fresno Bulldogs. A street gang, but they're connected to the Mexican mafia. Th-they supply our heroin, so when the girls overdosed, we called them, and they sent a few big Mexicans to clean everything up. That's what happened, and that's all I know, I *swear!*" Chad insisted, fighting the hysterical cries that wanted to rip from his throat.

"I think you know a little more," Petty stated while continuing to bag up the dope.

"I don't, I swear I don't," Chad replied vehemently.

"You know how to make contact and get some more of this dope. You do that, and it might save your life," Petty said.

I was already following his train of thought about shaking the drug pipeline, but we both knew he was lying to Chad. Chad was dead already.

"You wanna make that call, Chad?" I asked.

"Yes, yes, I'll call them, just don't shoot me."

"Make the call then," I instructed, pulling my gun away from his face and standing up.

It took Chad a couple minutes to get his phone out of his pocket and get himself under control enough to actually make the call, but he got it done. I listened closely to every word that he spoke to make sure he wasn't trying to set us up in anyway.

"Well?" I asked once he'd hung up.

"Miguel will be here in twenty with half a key of the same shit that's on the table," Chad replied.

"Good job," Petty said.

"You can let me go now."

Whatever plea he was getting ready to make was forever silenced by the three bullets that I pumped into his chest and the clean hole I added to his forehead with a final shot.

"You know that we could've got some *real* money out of him, right?" Petty asked, closing the now full Ziploc bag and tossing it into my duffle bag.

"This ain't about the money," I replied shortly.

I could tell by the look on my partner's face that even if he didn't like my position on this issue, he wasn't about to argue with it. Having some hundred million dollar type motherfuckers in our grasp was probably a once in a lifetime move, but you couldn't put a price on loyalty. If your loyalty was for sale, you'd ultimately end up paying the highest price.

"So what are the odds that we get the info we need out of this runner who's bringing the dope?" Petty asked.

"He probably won't know anything that could cripple the infrastructure of the Mexican mafia, but he'll know where the stash house is, and possibly who's in charge of Fresno."

"Is it my turn to have a little fun?" Petty asked, smiling.

"You should find whatever you need in the duffle bag."

By the time Petty got shit set up the way he wanted it, there was a knock on the hotel room's front door.

"I got it, bruh," I said, stepping aside and ushering the well-dressed man into the room.

I'd expected some kid covered in tattoos with his pants barely covering his ass, but the 6'7" Mexican had no visible tats, a tailored dark blue suit, and a man bun.

What he was wearing and the leather briefcase he was carrying definitely allowed him to blend in with the clientele of the Four Seasons. I'd simply been expecting something different. He entered the room without a word, heading towards the living room in a way that indicated his familiarity with the layout. When he turned the corner and spotted the dead bodies, though, he stopped in his tracks.

"Chad and Brad had appointments to keep, but we'd still like to discuss some business with you," I said calmly from behind him while jamming my gun into his spine.

"Do you know who you're fucking with?" Miguel asked calmly in an accent-free voice.

"Why don't you enlighten us," Petty said, beckoning Miguel forward with a wave of his gloved hand.

"All you need to know is that the people I work for will slaughter your entire families, even though the amount of dope you're about to take is insignificant. A half of a key is *nothing* to them, but is it worth your families' lives?" he asked seriously.

"Your employers already made a move against my family when they put out a product that killed two innocent girls that you helped dispose of," I replied.

"Hookers are not innocent, and it was their fault for - "

I swiftly smacked him in the back of the head with my pistol hard enough to fuck up his man bun, leave a gapping gash in his scalp, and force him to find his knees like he was searching for religion.

"I got him," Petty said, stepping forward and relieving Miguel of his briefcase.

When he passed me the briefcase, I took a seat in a chair next to the couch occupied by Brad's motionless corpse and opened it. Inside I found a Ziploc bag similar to the one Petty had used to put the dope in earlier, and it was full with what appeared to be the same substance. Next to it lay a pretty chrome Taurus .45 pistol.

"Nice gun," I said, setting mine on top of the dope and picking his up for a closer inspection.

Not surprisingly, there was no visible serial number, which was good for what I had in mind. While I wiped my own pistol clean of any fingerprints, Petty used zip ties to bind Miguel's hands and feet, and then he rolled him on his back.

"Okay, Miguel, we can do this the easy way or the hard way. We want to know everything that you know, and we don't have time to play games," Petty said, standing over him.

"I'm not telling you shit, so just kill me," Miguel replied calmly.

"Kill you? Not yet, amigo," Petty said, going to my duffle bag and retrieving the eight inch buck knife.

Miguel's tough guy façade remained intact, but the look of concern in his eyes couldn't be masked.

"I know you were taught to keep your mouth shut no matter what, but I gotta be honest with you, Miguel, it's only gonna make your situation worse. I won't lie to you, you're gonna die, but whether you experience unspeakable pain along the way is your decision," Petty said, approaching the bound man slowly with the knife out in front of him.

"If Brad and Chad could talk, they'd tell you that we ain't bullshitting," I chimed in.

"I ain't got shit to say," Miguel replied defiantly.

His response actually made Petty laugh, but the laugh wasn't one of humor. It was sinister. He demonstrated just how sharp the buck knife was by cutting Miguel's belt off, and then cutting a slit down the front of the now-trembling man's slacks.

"I wouldn't move if I was you," Petty advised, smiling.

Once he had a nice hole cut thru the fabric of the pants, he pulled another zip tie from his pocket. I could tell by the expression on Miguel's face that he had no idea what was about to happen, but he was about to learn. As quick as a snake charmer, Petty reached inside Miguel's pants, pulled his dick through the hole, slid the zip tie over it, and pulled it tight.

"What the fuck!" Miguel yelled, struggling uselessly to get away.

"Don't worry, I didn't cut off the circulation, which means you'll be able to feel *every bit* of what happens next," Petty replied.

"Wait, wait, man, you don't have to do that," Miguel protested.

The screeching sound of his voice shattered any illusions of him being calm, and indicated that he might not want to go down this road.

"Who do you work for?" I asked.

"Pl-please, man, you know I can't tell you anything. If I do, they'll kill me."

"You obviously weren't listening to what I told you earlier," Petty said, taking a firm hold of Miguel's dick and pressing the huge blade of the buck knife into the middle of it. Miguel's screams started off low, but as Petty broke skin and began dragging the blade towards the head of his dick, he sounded off like an opera audition.

"I'ma split this motherfucker like a cooked sausage if you don't start talking," Petty promised.

"Okay! Okay! Okay!" Miguel yelled quickly.

"Talk fast," I said from my seat.

"I'm a Bulldog. We get our p-product straight from Mexico, but I don't know who controls shit down there. Out supplier for all of Cali is a guy named Saint. That's all I know," Miguel replied.

"What's Saint look like and where can we find him?" I asked.

"I've never fucking seen him, man! I'm just a mule!" he insisted.

"Where's the main stash house?" Petty asked.

"6264 Imperial Avenue, but it's guarded at all times by at least ten Bulldog members. It's suicide to try to rob that place," Miguel replied.

"Let us worry about that. You got any more questions for him?" Petty asked, looking over at me.

I thought about it for a minute, but ultimately I knew that the answers I needed would have to come from someone higher up.

"No, I'm good," I said.

Petty quickly cut the zip tie from around Miguel's dick, but instead of letting it go and putting the knife away, he jammed the blade into the base of Miguel's dick and swiftly sliced him from bottom to top. Suddenly Miguel's favorite body part resembled a rare steak, and the wails coming from his mouth indicated his feelings about that. After a long, agonizing thirty seconds, I stood up to put a bullet in Miguel's head with his own gun, but Petty stopped me.

"Let him bleed out. It'll be more painful that way," Petty said.

I nodded my head in approval, which was all Petty needed to separate Miguel from his dick forever.

"You gonna stuff it in his mouth now?" I asked.

"Nah, we ain't Italian. I'll just leave it right here by his head so he can fill it up with his tears."

135

"You're sick," I replied, chuckling.

"Thank you."

The abrupt stop of Miguel's screams indicated that the pain he was in was too much to bear. I didn't know if he would regain consciousness before he bled out and died, but I knew we wouldn't be here. Petty quickly cleaned up and packed up everything we needed, and then I made a call down to the manager of the Four Seasons. After I was assured that a proper, thorough, cleaning would take place, it was time for us to vanish as quietly as we'd come.

"So what's next?" Petty asked once we were back in the car, creeping through the sleepy Fresno streets.

"Now we find a place to sleep because at sunrise, we go back to it. We're just getting started."

Chapter 15

"Detective Pettybone, Detective Cooper, I'm Detective Josh Morgan, Narcotics. How can I help you?" he asked, shaking each of our hands before resuming his seat behind his desk.

Morgan was a short-built white man with a receding hairline, badly-stained teeth, and even worse breath, but in Fresno, he was the man we needed to see. I nodded towards Petty, who put the briefcase on Morgan's desk, opened it, and turned it towards him.

"We've come all the way from Vegas because two working girls overdosed on this almost pure heroin. The girls were found in Oakland, but they actually died in Fresno," I said.

"How much of this story do I want to know?" Morgan asked pointedly.

"We'll give you the highlights. This product is coming directly out of Mexico, and the Fresno Bulldogs are distributing it out here. We've got the location of their main stash house out here, but I'll warn you now that it's heavily guarded, so you'll want to go in hot and heavy," I said.

"Understood. What is it that you want out of this?" Morgan asked.

"Our concern is ultimately the supplier because this product can't continue to be put out or consumed, or more people will die. We have reason to believe that someone named Saint is responsible for the distribution of heroin for all of California, and he's doing this on behalf of the Mexican mafia," I replied.

The mention of the name Saint caused a noticeable shift in Morgan's demeanor, and one look at Petty told me that he'd noticed the same thing.

"Saint, huh?" Morgan asked softly.

"How much of this story do *we* want to know?" Petty asked.

"All of it probably, but it's best that we don't discuss any more of this in the station. Let's go grab some lunch - your treat," Morgan replied, standing up and grabbing his wrinkled, shit brown suit jacket to match the slacks he was wearing.

Petty closed the briefcase and we followed Morgan's lead out of the police station.

"I know a nice diner not far from here. Follow me," Morgan instructed, heading for his car.

"I got a bad feeling," I said to Petty as we made our way towards my car.

"We came to get answers, right?" Petty asked.

I knew he was right, but that didn't get rid of the uneasiness I was feeling. We got in the car, and after a short ten minute drive, we arrived at a spot called Lunchbox.

"Put the dope in the trunk," I said before we got out.

Once that was done, we followed Morgan inside and sat in the booth across from him. It didn't escape my attention that he'd chosen a noisy, populated place to eat, or that we were sitting in the back far enough from anyone eavesdropping. There was a thin line between paranoid and cautious, and Detective Morgan was flirting with it.

"The crab cakes here are amazing," Morgan raved, looking around inconspicuously.

We all placed our order when the short, redheaded waitress came around, but no other words were spoken until she'd disappeared.

"It doesn't surprise me that the road you're traveling leads to Saint, but you should know that chasing him is like trying to catch the wind with your bare hands," Morgan stated calmly.

"You make him sound like the boogie man," Petty replied.

138

"Hunting the boogie man would be easier, I'm afraid," Morgan said seriously.

"Tell us what you know," I said.

"Fabian 'Saint' Santord was born in East L.A thirty-five years ago to a prostitute that got rid of him before she passed the placenta through her pussy. Saint grew up on the streets and earned a reputation as brutal very early on, which made him a prime target for recruitment by LA EME. The Mexican mafia. He has little formal education, but possesses a high I.Q. Couple that with a short fuse and a long memory, and you can understand why he's no one to fuck with. He's been suspected of no less than thirteen homicides by his own hand, and the number of deaths he's ordered are immeasurable," Morgan said.

"How is he still a free man?" I asked.

"Money and power buy freedom in courts around the country every day. California is no different, sadly," Morgan replied, shaking his head.

"I'm assuming someone like you're describing has local law enforcement on his payroll, but what about the Feds?" Petty asked.

"Honestly, I'm not sure how long Saint's reach is, but law enforcement that has gone after him has a way of disappearing. As far as I can tell he only has one weakness - if you can call it that," Morgan replied.

"Who is she?" I asked.

To this question Morgan pulled his phone from his pocket and began searching for something. After a few minutes, he turned the phone towards us to see.

"The huge cholo with all the tattoos is Saint, and the female standing beside him is - "

"Sophia," I said weakly.

I could feel both men's eyes on me, but mine remained locked on the screen as my mind tried to convince itself that I wasn't seeing what I was seeing.

"Sophia, as in...?" Petty said, asking me the one question that I didn't want to answer.

Petty knew a lot about my past, but only a little about Sophia. All he knew for sure was that she was important to me once upon a time.

"I get the feeling that I'm missing something," Morgan said, pulling his phone back and breaking the spell that Sophia's picture had me under.

She'd transformed from beautiful to gorgeous since the last time I'd seen her, but her eyes had gone the opposite way. There was no beauty in them, but the darkness was easy to spot.

"Sophia Dettger is what exactly to Saint?" I asked calmly.

"Her name is Sophia Santoro, and she's Saint's wife. They also have a son together. She may be beautiful, but she's as ruthless as her husband, and fiercely loyal. At one point it was thought she could be used against Saint, but no one has ever gotten close enough to test that theory. There's definitely blood under those manicured nails," Morgan stated.

"Is she involved in Saint's business?" Petty asked.

"Absolutely, but she maneuvers with the precision and patience of a black widow. To my knowledge, no one has gotten close to prosecuting her for anything. The question I need answered is how do *you* know her?" Morgan asked.

Our conversation was interrupted by the arrival of our food, and I used the momentary distraction to figure out what I was gonna say.

"Long story short, our paths have crossed before," I replied, chewing my crab cake slowly.

"And?" Morgan prodded.

"And that's it. What we need to focus on now is shutting her husband down, because the heroin he's putting out is ninety-seven percent pure and incredibly lethal," I replied.

"Do you have any suggestions on how to solve the problem you're describing?" Morgan asked half-sarcastically.

"I'm not criticizing what's been done already, Detective, but I do think two new sets of eyes could go a long way towards seeing things differently. Would it be possible to have whatever info you have on the Santoro's?" I asked.

"Give me your number," Morgan replied without hesitation.

I recited my cell phone number for him and he immediately went about tapping on his phone's screen. I could feel Petty nudging me under the table, but I ignored that and his pointed stare and continued to eat my crab cakes with my side of French fries. To anyone observing I appeared to be nothing more than a customer enjoying his meal, but inwardly, I was screaming my goddamn head off! If I thought that Deliah telling me I'd called Sophia's name out in my sleep had brought my past rushing back, it was nothing compared to the new info I was trying to process. The amount of questions that I had was threatening to fry every circuit in my brain, but somehow, I still managed to stay calm.

"Alright, I just sent you a copy of the file we have on Saint. It's interesting reading, but you didn't get it from me," Morgan said, giving us knowing looks.

"We appreciate that, and to show our appreciation, we'd like to turn over the heroin in our possession to you. We're in your jurisdiction, and it should be known that you're responsible for cleaning up these streets," I replied.

"In that case, lunch is on me," Morgan said, smiling.

Somehow I managed to engage in idle chitchat and even swap a few on the job stories for the next twenty minutes, when all I really wanted to do was run. Fuck the crab cakes, fuck the man paying for them. I just wanted to slide out of the booth and make a mad dash for the door. Instead, I showed the proper amount of interest in what Detective Morgan was saying and the proper amount of appreciation for the good food. At the end of the meal, Morgan settled the check and we all went out to my car.

"Thanks for all your help," I said, handing him the briefcase from my trunk.

"Likewise. Keep me posted and let me know if there's anything that I can do," Morgan replied.

We all shook hands and then went our separate ways.

"So, I'm gonna assume that the Sophia who was in that picture with the Mexican Incredible Hulk is the same one you grew up with," Petty said as soon as we got in the car.

"Yeah," I replied shortly, starting the engine and speeding out of the diner's parking lot.

My next destination was unclear, but I knew that I wanted to get there fast.

"Talk to me, bruh," Petty said after five minutes of me zigzagging thru traffic at high rates of speed.

"It's complicated."

"Yeah, I gathered that much back at the diner. I think you need to tell me what I don't know because it's obvious that whatever it is, is eating at you," Petty said, sounding concerned.

I trusted Pettybone with my life, but it was beyond hard to trust anybody with my past. Ordinarily this wasn't something I'd have to worry about, but it wasn't hard to tell my past and future were now on a collision course.

"Sophia was my right hand when I was coming up. She was the only person that I truly trusted."

"Obviously something changed," Petty replied.

"The product that we're chasing is the same shit that killed my mother ten years ago, and it was me and Sophia who helped put it in the streets where we come from."

"Ooooh, fuck," Petty said slowly.

When I looked over at him, I could see that he understood how crazy all of this was, and he didn't even know the whole story. Nor would he know the whole story. We rode on in silence until we reached the Super 8 motel we'd checked into.

"So what's our next move?" Petty asked before we got out of the car.

"I need some time to figure that out, bruh, but right now, I just want to stare at the ceiling until shit makes sense again."

"Well head on into the room then. I'll meet you in there after I run to the lobby real quick," Petty said.

I did as he suggested, going straight for the closest bed and falling flat on my back. The one question that kept swimming relay laps in my mind was how the fuck had I gotten here? It felt like I was trapped in some type of alternate universe because never could I have imagined Sophia and I being on opposite ends of a life or death situation. What was my next move? No matter how many times or how many different ways I asked myself that same question, I always ran into a mental brick wall, and it was starting to piss me off.

"Here, this should help you focus," Petty said, coming into the room a few minutes later and tossing a bag of gummy bears on my chest.

"I know it's the thought that counts, but this ain't a little kid problem that can be cured with candy."

"Look a little closer," Petty replied cryptically.

When I looked at the package of gummy bears in my hand, I saw what I'd missed the first time, the weed leaf that indicated that this particular sweet treat was an edible full of THC.

"Maybe candy will help," I conceded, opening the package and popping a fistful of gummy bears into my mouth.

It took me less than five minutes to finish the entire bag, and it wasn't long after that when I felt my mind expand in a familiar, comforting way.

"I forgot how much I love bud," I said slowly.

"Me too," Petty replied, snickering.

With every minute that passed, I found myself relaxing more and more until eventually, I felt like a warm rainbow all over.

"It wasn't just business between you and her, was it?" Petty asked suddenly.

"Nah. Sophia was my best friend. Then some crazy shit happened and our friendship became more."

"You talking about your moms overdosing, huh?" Petty asked softly.

"Nah, it was before that. My mom got shot while a trap house she was in was being robbed. Sophia and I were the ones pulling the heist, and I was the one who dropped the hammer on my moms," I replied matter-of-factly.

There was complete silence following my statement except for the sounds of Petty's smacking as he ate his gummy bears.

"Damn, bruh, you've been carrying a lot of shit on your shoulders that I didn't know nothing about. Why didn't you tell me?" he asked.

"Ever since all that shit happened I've been focusing on remembering how to forget, but that shit is impossible now. I became a cop as a legal means to hustle with longevity and success that average street niggas fail to attain. I also did it to one day find the manufacturer of that killer dope that still haunts me, and now after all these years, the chase is on again. I gotta destroy everybody involved with this heroin and its distribution. Maybe that's the only way I'll ever be able to open my eyes in the morning and not feel guilt for my mother not being able to do the same."

Petty took a seat on the bed next to mine and tossed me another bag of gummy bears. I opened them, but instead of demolishing them like I did the first bag, I chewed them one at a time thoughtfully. I knew being high wouldn't improve the situation I'd found myself in, but it did allow me to accept my new reality a little easier.

"You know you my nigga, and nothing that you've told me will change that. It sounds like you're preparing to saddle up and ride into hell, and you better know that I'm going with you," Petty declared.

"Ride into hell, huh? Yeah, that's *exactly* what I'm about to do, but I'm going after the devil I know. I'm going after Sophia."

ASAD

Chapter 16
Two days later
Los Angeles

"There she is," I said, nodding towards the front of the restaurant that Sophia had just come out of.

"And she's not alone," Petty replied.

It was clear to see that the two body builder type white guys surrounding her were there for security purposes, which was something I hadn't expected to find. The Sophia I had known didn't need security. It was everyone else that needed protection from her. I'd studied all the information Detective Morgan had passed on about Fabian "Saint" Santoro, which included info on Mrs. Santoro and her habits. Nothing was mentioned about how she traveled under the protection of armed guards.

"This makes snatching her off the street a little harder," Petty said, looking over at me.

"Not really. I mean, we knew where she'd be eating lunch because this is her usual spot on Tuesdays, but the streets of downtown L.A. are still too busy to get away with a daytime abduction. So we improvise."

"What do you have in mind?" Petty asked.

"Let's see what her next move is."

No sooner had I said that then one of her minions stepped to an all-black Lincoln Navigator parked at the curb and opened the door for Sophia to climb in. Once she was in, they loaded up and pulled off into the swiftly flowing traffic, causing me to start the engine of my car and follow their lead.

"You got any idea where she's headed next?" Petty asked.

"No. Her son doesn't get out of school for another two and a half hours, so she could be up to anything, especially with Saint being out of town."

"He still up in Fresno snooping around?"

"Yep. The Dobs brothers were big money clients and their death puts a nice hole in quite a few people's pockets. Not to mention what happened to your friend Miguel, and the dope that came up missing. Oh, and let's not forget the main stash house in Fresno that got steamrolled by Detective Morgan and the entire narcotics division. I'd say that Saint will be busy for a while," I replied, smirking.

"That could explain why the little lady is so protected. Saint feels like he's under attack."

"You *did* split a man's dick open like you were gonna put relish and mustard on the motherfucker. There might not have been any footage of us or anyone else in the room, but it was obvious that Miguel was tortured," I stated honestly.

Petty's chuckles showed his lack of remorse for what he'd done, but I didn't mind. If I had my way, shit would be getting uglier in the near future. I continued to follow the SUV at a discreet distance until it pulled into the parking lot of a local tattoo shop, forcing me to pull into the Starbucks across the street.

"You think she plans to spend the next couple hours in there?" he asked.

"Only one way to find out, I guess," I replied, reaching into the center console and grabbing the chrome Taurus .45 that used to belong to Miguel.

"Tell me we're not about to shoot up the whole tattoo shop," he said seriously.

"You don't want to have any fun today? Fine, we'll just go in, flash our badges, and take Sophia in for questioning."

"The only problem I see with that is that we're way out of our jurisdiction, and I'm pretty sure that your girl is smart enough to know that," he replied.

"You're right, she is smart enough to know that, but she'll be too shocked at seeing me to focus on that part of it. Plus I'm counting on the distraction I'm gonna cause to work in our favor."

"Why did I get chills when you just said that?" he asked.

It was my turn to chuckle as I tucked the gun into the waist of my jeans and climbed out of the car.

"She's probably in the back by now. We're playing this by ear because we have no idea how many people are inside, so keep your eyes open," I said as we crossed the street at a casual stroll.

"I got your back."

I could see one of the two guards sitting in the tattoo waiting area through the window, and I nodded towards Petty so he knew to move on him when necessary.

"Hi, welcome to Ink Blast, do you have an appointment?" the bubbly blonde receptionist asked.

"No, no appointment, I'm just meeting someone. Can you tell me where Sophia Santoro is?" I asked politely.

Just like I'd anticipated, the mention of Sophia's name immediately got the attention of her hired help, and he jumped to his feet. Before he could get to the pistol he was reaching for, Petty fired a left-right combination that had him snoozing up against the receptionist desk.

"Shhhh," I said, putting a finger to my lips while pulling my badge out to show the frightened woman staring wide-eyed at me.

"Where is she?" I whispered.

"In-in the back. Third cubicle on your left."

"Petty, keep your eyes on sleeping beauty and get the video surveillance," I said, making my way further into the tattoo shop.

I waited until I was out of the receptionist's sight before I pulled the pistol out, but I kept it concealed behind my back as I slowly rounded the corner into the spacious cubicle. Sophia was relaxed in the tattoo chair with her eyes closed while a short, Spanish guy was drawing a stencil on her left arm. Her security was sitting right by the entrance, but he didn't move quickly enough when he saw me to prevent coming forehead to barrel with my gun. I shook my head slowly so he would understand that any sudden movements would be bad for his life's expectancy.

"What does your pussy taste like?" I asked.

The way Sophia jumped in the chair and her eyes flew open would've made someone think I'd shot her, but as her look of shock transformed to one of complete coldness, someone would've thought that she wanted to shoot me.

"How my pussy tastes is none of your business, and my husband wouldn't like you asking such a disrespectful question," she replied tightly.

"Do you really believe that I care about what your husband *likes*, Sophia? You know me better than that," I said, smiling.

"I know that you're a dead man if you don't get that gun off of my employee and leave before you piss me off," she replied, smiling in a way that didn't quite reach her eyes.

"A dead man, huh? Why don't you tell me how you *really* feel," I said.

"I don't feel anything for you other than annoyance. Now leave, and that's the last time I'm gonna make you that offer," she replied, closing her eyes and leaning back in the tattoo chair.

For a second I could only stare at her, trying to wrap my mind around this woman I once knew like the back of my hand. I'd never known her to be so dismissive, but she was about to learn real quick that I was still the wrong nigga to fuck with.

"Get out of the chair and come quietly, Sophia. I don't want to hurt you."

"Even if you didn't know who my husband is, and I know you do, you *still* couldn't hurt me. You ain't built like that," she replied, looking at me with a direct challenge in her eyes.

I didn't respond verbally, but I did smile genuinely at her. Then I pulled the trigger and put her bodyguard's thoughts all over the cubicle wall.

"My apologies for the ruined artwork," I said, addressing the now-trembling tattoo artist.

"It's-it's cool, I didn't like that mural anyway," he replied.

"Shall we?" I asked Sophia, gesturing towards the exit.

I could see the defiance in her, but I'd definitely gotten her attention enough to have her moving out of the tattoo chair and grabbing her purse.

"I'll carry that for you," I offered, quickly removing the bag from her grip.

I could tell by how heavy it was that there was a gun inside, but that didn't surprise me.

"You're gonna regret this," Sophia said under her breath as she walked past me.

"I doubt that, but the day is still young," I replied, following closely behind her.

By the time we got to the front of the shop, I'd tucked my gun back out of sight so the receptionist wouldn't see it, but I was worried about nothing.

"What did you do?" I asked Petty, looking around.

"Suggested that she take an early lunch. The real question is, what did *you* do?" Petty asked.

"You're a cop? Arrest this man, because he just shot my bodyguard," Sophia said, moving quickly to Petty's side.

I couldn't stop laughing.

"It's funny until your black ass ends up on death row, you — "

She bit off the rest of her statement as her eyes locked in on the badge I was waving in her face.

"You've gotta be *fucking* with me," she said in disbelief.

"It's okay. You have the right to remain silent," Petty said, taking her by the arm and guiding her out the front door of the shop.

To the casual observer we looked like three friends, but when we got to my car, I put handcuffs on Sophia before pushing her into the backseat.

"I'm guessing that she wasn't happy to see you," Petty said, going to the passenger side door.

"You think?" I replied sarcastically, climbing into the driver's seat.

"I want my fucking lawyer!" Sophia demanded.

"I'll get right on that, but we're gonna have a little chat first," I replied.

"Yeah, right. You try talking to me without my lawyer and your badge will be nothing more than a paperweight, nigga," she said seriously.

Instead of arguing with her, I started the car and put some distance between us and the tattoo shop, knowing that as soon as we left, the tattoo artist notified somebody. More than likely it would be someone who could get word to her husband in Fresno.

"Where we going?" Petty asked.

"I'd like to get back home court advantage, but that might be doing too much, so let's just go to the motel," I replied.

"What's the plan?" Petty asked.

When I looked over at him, I had every intention of lying just so he wouldn't lose faith in my ability to remain emotionless about this situation, but I couldn't find the words. Surprisingly, the look he gave me was one of understanding without judgment, and that told me that no words were necessary.

"I don't know what this is about, *Officer* Cooper, but I'm telling you that the best thing you can do for yourself is let me go. Saint ain't nobody you wanna fuck with and he loves me more than life itself," Sophia said.

"You think so, huh? I think he loves money and power just a little more importantly. Don't be dumb."

"Your sidekick know about Lilliana?" she asked sweetly.

"Sidekick? First of all, we're *detectives*, and more importantly, don't be dumb enough to think that you can cause distrust between us," Petty interjected.

"That wasn't my intention at all, *Detective*, I was simply wondering if your self-righteous partner told you about how he executed his pregnant girlfriend to keep business running smooth," she replied calmly.

She didn't know Petty well enough to know what his silences meant, but I knew that the words swimming through his mind right now were "what the fuck". The shock I felt about what Sophia had just revealed quickly turned to clear understanding about how we ended up in this situation.

"Is that what you think happened?" I asked, looking at her through the rearview mirror.

"That's what I *know*," she replied confidently.

It was clear to me that she and I had to have a long conversation in the near future so I could find out what else she *knew*. Without having to be asked or told, Petty turned on the radio and that effectively ended all conversation until I pulled up at the motel thirty minutes later.

"If you can handle that tiger in the backseat, I'll go grab us some food real quick," Petty offered.

"I'm good with that," I replied.

I gave Petty the car keys, got Sophia's purse and grabbed her out of the back, and marched her into the motel room.

"If this is about a quickie or some trip down memory lane, can you hurry up and fuck me so I can be on my way," she requested once we were alone in the room.

"You know like I do that I ain't never had to take no pussy, and I ain't about to start," I replied, pushing her down onto one of the two beds.

"So what the fuck do you want, Maxwell?"

"To talk to you," I replied, sitting across from her.

"To talk? *Now*? Nigga, you vanished on me a decade ago without a word or a backwards glance, but you want to talk *now*? Man, get the fuck out of here," she said angrily.

"I had to leave, Sophia. You know it and I know it. There was no way for me to stay after what happened to my mom."

"And you don't think I would've understood that if you had cared to explain? Shit, I would've left with you, but instead you threw me away like you did Lilliana," she said, screwing her face up in disgust.

"I can tell that you have selective amnesia about some things. Lilliana died because she put the police on you - or was the entire situation not fully explained when Brewer brought you in to fill my spot? Don't look surprised that I know that. It's the only thing that makes logical sense. He was the only witness to what went down with Lilliana, and the fact that you ended up married to the West Coast plug for the killer dope we had can't be a coincidence. I just wish I'd known sooner because I would've made him suffer more before I killed him."

"Y-you killed Brewer?" she asked, shocked.

"Of course I did. It was his fault that we even had access to a product that pure, which made him partially responsible for what happened to my mom."

It only took a few seconds for the light of realization to dawn clearly in her eyes, and suddenly I saw some of her anger vanish.

"Th-that's why you left me, ain't it? You never wanted any part of the dope game, and if you blamed Brewer, then you *definitely* blamed me too. So why didn't you kill me?" she asked.

"You know why I didn't kill you, Sophia."

"No, I don't know why, so explain it to me," she insisted.

When I'd confronted her in the tattoo shop earlier her eyes had been like a one way mirror, but now I could see through her, and beneath her anger was pain. I didn't want to care about that, especially since she was literally sleeping with the enemy, but I knew I wasn't looking at the woman she'd grown into. I was seeing the girl from my past.

"I didn't kill you because I loved you," I said softly.

I don't know what words I expected from her following my declaration, but she didn't give me none. At first all she did was shake her head slowly back and forth like she was calling me a liar. Then the tears came. She didn't cry hysterically or cuss me out while wailing from somewhere deep in her soul, but her silent tears had the same effect of making me feel some type of way.

"Sophia, I - "

"Shut up, Max, I don't want to hear it," she said.

"I'm just trying to explain."

"I don't want your explanation. I'm good. If you loved me, you should've at least talked to me, but it doesn't matter because I know that there's no way you feel anything other than hate for me now," she replied.

"I don't hate you, Sophia."

"Sure you do. Not only did I help put your mom in the ground, but I then married the plug! You've gotta hate me because right about now *I* hate me," she said passionately.

"I don't hate you, Sophia, I swear."

"Okay then, prove it. Don't kill me. For the sake of our son, don't kill me."

Chapter 17

"Repeat what you said," I requested, figuring that I'd heard her wrong.

"You wouldn't believe me if I did, so I'll show you. Get my purse."

I didn't know what type of trickery she was trying to pull, but my curiosity got the best of me and I retrieved her purse from the table I'd tossed it on.

"Nice pistol," I said, taking the snub-nosed .357 Smith and Wesson and putting it in my pocket.

"That's not what I wanted you to get. I want you to get my phone."

"Okay, and?" I replied, pulling it out.

"I'm pretty sure you've seen a picture of Saint, but if not, there's a few of him in there, along with pictures of my son. See for yourself."

I looked at her long and hard, searching for any signs of deception, but not finding any didn't make me feel better. It scared me. Still, I took a deep breath and began to slowly swipe through her phone gallery until I came upon the first picture of her little boy. Seeing him caused my heart to stop momentarily, because I'd seen him before. It had been more than fifteen years ago though, and I'd been looking in a mirror.

"There's no way he's my son," I said softly.

"I can hear the denial in your voice, but you're only lying to yourself. He's your son, Max."

"Saint wouldn't - "

"He *did* raise another man's child because I kept it real with him from the beginning. Well, for the most part. I was introduced to him about three months after you got ghost, and I told him that my child's father was dead. Without hesitation, he offered to step in and step up, but I kept him at arm's length because I was hoping that you'd come back. When you didn't..."

She didn't have to finish the rest of her sentence because the rest was history. I still had questions though.

"Did Brewer know the truth?" I asked.

"Yeah, he did. A couple weeks after you left, he came to me with a business proposition that I couldn't refuse and we formed a business relationship. When the time came that I couldn't hide my pregnancy anymore I told him everything and begged him to help me find you. That's when he told me exactly what happened with Lilliana in that basement, and he convinced me that the best thing for me and my unborn child was to forget you."

"And you listened?" I asked.

"What was I supposed to think, Max? You were gone! Did you want me to alienate the only motherfucker helping me to provide for our son? I didn't have the luxury of living life with my heart instead of my head, but I did love you, Maxwell. I still do."

My brain felt like it would explode at any moment from all the information I was trying to process, forcing me to sit back on the bed before I fell down. I wanted to scream at her and call her every name that I could think of, but the truth was that this was my fault. All of this was my fault.

"Wh-what's his name?" I asked, looking at the mocha brown face with my features on her phones screen.

"Angelo. His name is Angelo Maxwell Santoro."

Part of me wanted to snap because she'd given my son another motherfucker's last name, but I would've been irrational to do so. Saint was her husband, and he was the only father that Angelo knew. I was just the sperm donor.

"Angelo," I said softly.

"He reminds me of you more and more each day!"

"Oh yeah? Do you tell him that, or does he believe Saint is his real father?" I asked, tasting the bitterness and anger on my tongue.

"Max, don't do this, don't make me justify and impossible decision," she replied, standing up and stepping towards me.

I was losing the battle with my anger and my tears, and her closeness was only serving to stir the emotional turmoil within me. When I looked up into her hazel eyes, she brought her bound hands to my face and stared at me the way no woman had since her.

"He's our son, and he was created in love. He's the reason that I've never stopped loving you, and I never will," she said, slowly bringing her face closer to mine until our lips were touching.

As gentle as the kiss was, it was still enough to rattle my brain harder than a boxer's punch. When Sophia pulled back I expected her to sit back on the bed opposite me, but instead, she did the unthinkable. While looking me dead in the eyes, she reached beneath her white summer dress, pulled her matching panties down, and casually stepped out of them. She then straddled me, putting her handcuffed wrists around my neck.

"This is a bad idea," I said.

"It never was before, was it?"

Before I could answer she pulled my mouth to hers, and this time our kiss wasn't gentle. It was filled with the fire you could only find in hell. There was nothing in me that could resist what was happening, and after a few moments I forgot any reason's to try. I laid her phone on the bed beside us and wrapped my arms around her. Pulling us soul to soul as time stood still, and then rewound.

"Put your dick in me," she demanded huskily before biting my neck hard enough to send shockwaves to my toes.

I quickly reached between us, unzipped my jeans to allow my throbbing dick to spring free, and then grabbed two handfuls of her juicy ass cheeks to guide her home. From the moment of penetration we became the perfect storm, and the ride was rough.

"Damn, you're tight," I panted, pulling her down on me harder with each stroke like I was trying to break the mold.

"J-just how y-you like it," she replied, rocking against me with the same intensity.

I knew she hadn't cum yet, but I could feel her pussy gushing like someone had turned the water on, and that only fed the insatiable growing hunger in me. There was no denying it; I needed more. Without warning I stood up with her in my arms and put her on her back on the opposite bed, diving deeper inside her than she was ready for. She took it though. With every pounding blow I delivered I could see the honey color of her eyes changing, getting darker, and I knew that signaled the building of her internal tsunami.

"Max-Max-Maxwell!" she screamed.

She was fighting to fuck me back as I tried to hammer her through the bed. The sound of her voice sounded like sweet submission, causing me slam into her harder. Within minutes she exploded all over me, whimpering weakly, but still begging me not to stop. Her pussy grip was like a vise on my throbbing dick and with each stroke, I could see my beautiful death a little clearer.

"L-let me r-ride you," she stammered breathlessly.

Part of me wanted to let her do just that, but I know she was just trying to take control of the situation. Instead of complying with her request I wrapped my arms around her, picked her up as I stood up, and carried her to the table that sat in the corner.

"Max, what are you - "

"Shut up," I growled, grabbing her by the throat and squeezing hard with every serving of dick I gave her.

Her eyes blazed with raw desire and long forgotten passion that she was remembering clearly. When she locked her legs around my waist her pussy's grip got tighter, and so did my grip on her throat. I could hear in her breathing that I was affecting her air supply past the point of sexy, but I saw no flare in her eyes, only determination.

"Cum!" she demanded, lifting her hips off of the table to meet my determined blows forcefully.

In my mind it was as defiant as always, but we both knew that she wasn't mentally fucking me. This was emotional warfare.

"C-cum in me, Maxwell," she demanded again.

Even as I opened my mouth to tell her no, I could feel my dick pulsating uncontrollably, and I knew that I was helpless to stop this moving train.

"Fuck!" I yelled, cumming inside her tight inferno, barely maintaining my balance.

Before my body could stop trembling I felt Sophia jump the last hurdle of her own climax, leaving us both breathless and wearing expressions of awe. It took me a few seconds to realize that I was still choking her, but when I did I quickly pulled my hand away and tried backing up.

"Stop running, Max," she said, tightening her legs around my waist, which kept my dick inside her.

"I'm not running, but Petty will be back any minute."

"Oh, so he doesn't know exactly how close we were back in the day?" she asked, smiling.

"No, and it's not his business," I replied, pulling us apart and fixing my clothing.

I sat down in the chair at the table, trying to make sense of everything that had just happened, but I couldn't keep a straight thought in my head.

"For what it's worth, I know that if you'd known that I was pregnant you wouldn't have abandoned me," she said.

I didn't detect any sarcasm in her voice, but I still looked her in the eyes to make sure.

"So was me cumming in you now a way for you to bring us back together, or further complicate matters?"

"Neither. I guess I just got caught up in the moment and the memory of what we used to have. Don't worry though, I won't be getting pregnant again," she replied.

"You sure about that?"

"Yes, Max, I'm on birth control."

"Birth control? Well, I guess I can understand Saint not wanting to have kids considering his chosen profession," I said sarcastically.

"And you're in a position to judge, right? I may not have seen you in ten years, but I know damn well you ain't no cop because you believe in law and order. You just killed a man in cold blood, and *then* fucked a woman that you kidnapped, so you probably shouldn't throw stones from your glass house."

"Yeah, whatever. It don't matter what I do, I still ain't caused the destruction that your husband has. You know it and I know it," I replied, looking her dead in the eyes.

She held my stare for a few seconds before looking away, but I didn't press the point any further.

"Saint doesn't know that I'm on birth control. It was my decision. I didn't want more kids," she said softly.

I wasn't sure how to respond to that piece of information, but I wasn't given the opportunity because the door opened and in strolled Petty. I quickly stood up to help him with the food, needing a distraction from the emotionally charged air surrounding Sophia and I.

"Good, you two managed not to kill each other," Petty said, smiling.

"I'm just as surprised as you are," Sophia commented from behind me.

"I got us all burgers and fries. I hope that doesn't throw you off of your L.A. diet," Petty said, looking at Sophia.

"No worries, I'm a cheap date. Ain't that right, Max?" she asked.

Petty looked at me quizzically, but I shook it off and set the food on the table.

"Use one of the chairs," I said, motioning for her to move off of the table.

"You put me up here," she whispered, smiling at me as she scooted down.

Before I could respond, my eyes locked in on the puddle Sophia had left behind, but I didn't move fast enough to clean it up before Petty saw it.

"Uh, is that what I think it is?" Petty asked, looking directly at me.

"If you think it's a mixture of my pussy juices from multiple orgasms and Max's cum, then yeah, it's *exactly* what you think it is," Sophia replied, heading to the bathroom and closing the door behind her.

"She's lying, right?" Petty asked.

My response was to dig inside the McDonald's bag, grab some napkins, and clean up our indiscretion. Petty didn't ask the same question twice. Instead, he started unpacking the food and then sat down to eat. I followed his lead, but I know there was no getting around the explanation that it would have to give. Petty and I ate in silence, and after a few minutes, we were joined by Sophia.

"Can you take these handcuffs off me?" she asked, extending her wrists towards me.

"Not gonna happen," Petty replied.

Sophia didn't so much as chance in his direction, and neither did I as I pulled out my handcuff key and unhooked her. She rubbed her wrists vigorously before sitting on my lap and grabbing a double cheeseburger off the table. Apparently this was the final straw for Petty because he stopped eating and simply started at us.

"I think he's waiting on some answers, and I don't think saying that it's complicated will suffice," she said, taking a huge bite out of her burger.

One look into my partner's eyes told me that she was right.

"Sophia and I used to be...close," I said slowly.

"So I gathered," Petty replied sarcastically.

"You still like to dance around the difficult conversations, huh Max? I got you. Detective, Max and I were more than close. We were best friends in the street and in the bedroom. How and why we fell out *is* too complicated to go into, and it's only further complicated by the fact that he's my son's biological father. I'm sure he didn't tell you that, but that's only because he just found out himself a short while ago," Sophia stated calmly.

Petty's eyes immediately met mine, and they were swimming with questions.

"It's all true," I said.

"Wow, that's absolutely fucking *crazy*!" Petty replied, setting his sandwich down and looking back and forth between us.

"Tell me about it," I replied.

"I guess it could've been worse. She could hate you and refuse to help us. But now - "

"I don't hate Max. I love him. I still can't help you all though," Sophia said.

"You *can't* stay with him, and you know all the reasons why," I said, feeling confused.

"Max, he's my husband, which means that I'm his wife. I couldn't testify against him if I wanted to, and I don't want to," she replied.

"Wh-what?" I asked in disbelief.

"What do you think Saint would do to me if I betrayed him? What about what he'd do to Angelo, your son? Saint ain't somebody to be fucked with, not even by you. Besides, my hands ain't exactly clean," she confessed.

I hated that everything she'd said made logical sense, because I could no longer approach this situation logically. I had to get her and our son away from all this shit before it was too late. No matter what she said, Saint's days were numbered.

"I know I haven't known you long, and you obviously have your own history with Mad Max here, but I know him as well as I know myself. This situation with Saint was already personal *before* Max knew about you, so trust me when I tell you that he's not walking away from this," Petty stated.

Sophia put her burger down and turned in my lap to face me.

"Don't do this, Max. If Saint is going down, let someone else do it," she pleaded.

"I told you before, I'm not running. Not anymore."

ASAD

Chapter 18

"I know you won't hesitate when it comes to killing, but Max, Saint is connected to some real bad people. The kind of people who even scare me," Sophia said seriously.

"I can't keep letting him push his product, Sophia, If I do that then I'm no better than he is and everything I've done since my mother's death was for nothing," I replied.

"You can't let misplaced guilt get you killed," she said.

"There's a way for you to both get what you want. We don't have to take on Saint head to head. We can simply go at his supplier," Petty stated.

"That won't work either," Sophia replied quickly.

"Why not?" I asked, becoming more frustrated by her obvious loyalty to her husband. At first she didn't say anything, but the indecision in her eyes told me that she was trying to decide how much to say.

"Why not, Sophia?" I asked again.

"Because the connect is Saint's uncle. The whole organizational structure at the top is family, generations of blood relatives with blood on their hands from all around the world. I'm telling you, they run shit like the old Chinese triads," she replied.

"That don't scare us," Petty said.

"Well, it should. I've seen and heard shit that I wish I could forget, and the only reason that I'm alive is because I proved that I'm built for this type of life," she said seriously.

I didn't need to ask her what she meant because with the people she was describing, we all knew that there was only one way to prove yourself. Murder.

"I get what you're saying, but - "

"But you're gonna move against Saint anyway," she said, shaking her head sadly.

"We already did," Petty confessed.

"All you have to do is let me go and I'll think of something."

"He's not talking about us taking you," I said.

"Oh God, what the fuck have you done, Max?" she asked.

"We're the reason that your husband is in Fresno right now," Petty replied.

I could tell by the look that Sophia leveled at me that she was more than a little familiar with the details of what had happened to cause Saint to make the trip to Fresno.

"You motherfuckers really are crazy, huh?" she asked.

"We are, and thank you for saying so," Petty replied, picking his burger back up and biting it.

I could tell by the way that she was looking at me that she hadn't meant for her statement to be a compliment.

"Max, listen to me. Not a day passed that I haven't thought about your mom and everything that happened because that was a turning point in my life for two different reasons. I understand what's motivating you, but *please* don't start a war with these people," she begged.

"They're connected, I get that, but with the purity of the dope they're pushing, I'll have the entire United States government behind me. You've got a decision to make, and I know that you're intelligent enough to know that your survival depends on your ability to align yourself with the winning side. This war started a long time ago for me, and I'm gonna see it through, with or without your help," I replied sincerely.

"Yeah, what he said," Petty chimed in around a mouth full of French fries.

Sophia's eyes were filled with so many emotions, and even traces of regret, but I still didn't know what she was thinking in this moment. Nothing I'd said was easy to hear, and I knew that she was torn. I was just hoping that she made the right decision for both her and our son.

"Do you even have a plan, or are you gonna keep going at Saint half-cocked until he gets the upper hand?" she asked finally.

"Oh, we'll put a plan together. We just found out about Saint," Petty replied.

"How is that possible? Every cop in L.A. knows who Saint is, even the ones not on his payroll," Sophia said.

"We're not based out of L.A. We came out here from Vegas," I replied.

She quickly looked at Petty before turning her questioning eyes back to me.

"The motherfuckers who ended up dead in Fresno threw a party, and some girls that I knew were at that party. They overdosed on heroin because they were made to continue snorting it," I said.

"And you're out for vengeance, so it's a safe bet that these women were close to you, which of course struck a nerve. There really is no way to talk you out of this," she said defeatedly.

"No, there isn't," I admitted.

Sophia got up from my lap and began to slowly pace the length of the hotel room, obviously thinking hard about everything. I couldn't blame her, especially since I'd already turned her life upside down once before. The only advantage she had this time was that she could see the storm coming, but that still didn't change the fact that with the storm came destruction. Catastrophic destruction.

"I need time, Max," she said, stopping in front of me.

"How much time?" I asked.

"I don't know, I just need some time!" she replied, clearly agitated.

"Nothing about this is easy, and we get that, but shit is gonna hit the fan sooner rather than later," Petty said.

"He's right," I agreed.

"If you're talking about regular law enforcement, then that's fine, but I need you two to just slow down and let me think this shit through," she replied.

I looked at her long and hard before replying. "If Saint feels the slightest change in you, or - "

"He won't," she assured me quickly.

When I looked over at Petty, I could see some indecision on his face, but he nodded his head in agreement.

"How are you gonna explain today?" I asked.

"Give me my gun back," she said, holding her hand out.

For a split second I hesitated, but I still dug her pistol out of my pocket and passed it to her.

"I'll say it was a botched kidnapping, fire off a couple shots, and make up some story about how I got away. Is this room paid in cash?" she asked.

"Of course," Petty replied.

"Good. When you two leave, I'll call for the cavalry. What's your number?" she asked me, going to the bed and retrieving her phone.

I recited my number and a couple seconds later, I felt my phone vibrate in my pocket.

"I'll get in touch with you. Don't make contact with me first, Max. No matter how badly you want to," she instructed.

"I'm not making you any promises because if you take too long, I'm coming for you *and* my son," I vowed.

I could tell that she wanted to argue, but she knew that there was no point in it.

"I won't take too long," she said softly.

The rest of our communication was done non-verbally, both of us speaking of love's power and endurance.

"I'll pack us up," Petty offered, rising and moving away from the table.

When Sophia took my hand in hers and squeezed it, I felt the promise that she was making, but it didn't ease my anxiety.

"I left you once. I'm not doing that again," I said sincerely.

"I know," she replied, pulling me to my feet and into her embrace.

We held on to each other tightly, feeling like the only two people in the world. Once I saw that Petty had taken all of our shit to the car, I kissed Sophia on the forehead gently before moving my lips lower to hers. Our tongues spoke like not a day had passed without us being together. So much of me didn't want this moment to end, but I forced myself to pull back because I knew this wasn't the conclusion of Sophia and me. We'd just turned the page on the next chapter.

"Be safe," I said.

"You too. Before you go, though, I need to answer your question from earlier."

"What question?" I asked.

Her response was to unzip my pants, pull my dick out, and drop to her knees. Before I could utter a word she had me in her mouth, sucking and slurping my dick with a tornado force. I was rock hard within seconds, but just as quickly it was over, she was back on her feet, and her lips were attacking mine with a fierce hunger. Her kisses only made my dick harder to the point that it was throbbing in pain.

"There. Now you know what my pussy tastes like," she said, smiling as she pulled back and tucked my dick back inside my jeans.

"That's just *wrong*," I replied, struggling to zip my jeans without hurting myself in a different way.

Her instant laughter sent chills down my spine, but Petty's sudden reappearance meant I couldn't do any of the things I had in mind.

"You know I'm gonna get you back for that, right," I stated.

"I'm counting on it," she replied seductively.

I kissed her again quickly and then followed Petty out of the motel room door.

"You drive," I said, tossing him the keys and going to the passenger side of the car.

I could tell that he was surprised, but we both knew that I had some major thinking to do because complicated couldn't begin to describe my life anymore. When Petty climbed behind the wheel, he tossed two bags of edible gummy bears in my lap.

"Thanks," I said, wasting no time opening the first bag and popping several of the sweet treats into my mouth.

"You definitely need them more than I do," he replied, starting the car and pulling off.

I did my best to let the music playing on the radio push all thoughts from my mind until I felt the gummy weed bears take affect and relax me. Only then did I feel like it was safe to open my boxed-in thoughts and peek in. Before I could get too deep in thought, my phone started vibrating in my pocket. I pulled it out and came face to face with the same picture of Angelo that I'd been staring at in the motel room, along with a message from his mother.

"Damn, he looks just like you," Petty commented.

I knew the smile on my face was one of pride, but I was more focused on the words Sophia had sent. According to her, I was the second best thing that had ever happened to her, and together we'd created the first. Before I could respond to her, she fired another picture, forcing me to turn my phone away from Petty's view because the pussy was for my eyes only, according to her. And it was a pretty pussy too. We exchanged a few texts, but sooner than I wanted we had to put a stop to it so she could step back into her life. We both made promises that we had every intention of keeping, and then just like that, she was gone.

"You okay?" Petty asked once I'd put my phone away.

"Not at all, bruh, and honestly, I don't even know if I will be when the smoke clears."

"You'll figure it out, my nigga, and you know that I'm with you every step of the way," he said reassuringly.

"I know, and I appreciate it because the only thing I know with absolute certainty right now is that motherfucker Saint gotta die. It's the only way that Sophia and my son will be free and not have to look over their shoulders."

"If that's what you want for Sophia and your son, then you need to go into this situation with your eyes wide open. Killing Saint is only the beginning if you want to protect what you love because his family is gonna swear vengeance in blood," Petty replied.

"I know that, and that's why I've gotta kill him without it pointing at you, me, or Sophia."

"Facts. I've been meaning to ask you, though, how much are you gonna tell Deliah?" Petty asked seriously.

Of all the questions that I knew needed answers, that was one that I wanted to avoid the most.

"I don't know."

All Petty could do was shake his head because he knew I was telling the truth. I quickly smashed my remaining gummy bears, leaned my seat back, and tried to find the answers to life's mysteries on the back of my eyelids. When Petty finally brought the car to a stop in the precinct parking lot several hours later, I still wasn't any closer to knowing what to say to Deliah.

"I'll bring the captain up to speed before I go home, and I'll call you in the morning," Petty said.

"Cool, wish me luck."

"Good luck," he replied, getting out of my car.

Once I was behind the wheel, I headed straight for Deliah's house, knowing that it would be some weak nigga shit to put this conversation off. I wasn't sure who all was in the house with her, so I texted her to come outside once I was sitting out front. Seeing her beautiful body glide towards me with flawless grace made me want to throw her on the hood of my car and fuck her like I missed her. That would have to wait though. Within seconds, she was sliding into the passenger seat beside me and throwing her arms around my neck while hugging me tight.

"I missed you, Max. I'm glad you're back," Deliah said sincerely.

"I missed you too, sweetheart."

"What's wrong?" she asked, pulling back and looking me in the eye.

"Everything is crazy, but I'll start with the biggest shock that I've had to deal with."

"Max, you're scaring me," she said softly.

"I can't tell you not to be, but right now, I just need you to listen and hear me out completely. I'll start with Sophia. I was just with her."

Chapter 19
Three weeks later

"Did you sleep at all?" Deliah asked, coming up behind me and wrapping her arms around my waist.

"I got a few hours."

"You need more than that, Max," she said with concern in her voice.

I knew she was right, but I kept my eyes focused out the huge picture window on the slowly rising sun instead of responding. It wasn't like I was intentionally going without sleep. It was just that every time I closed my eyes I saw Sophia's face, and that made sleep impossible. I'd told Deliah almost everything that had happened with Sophia while I was in L.A., but I couldn't speak of the renewed emotional connection. I had to carry that, and the guilt I felt for betraying Deliah, by myself. This situation wasn't like when I'd been fucking both Sophia and Lilliana. This was different because my connection with Deliah was deeper than puppy love. At the same time, my life was for too complicated for a love triangle. It had been more than a week since I'd heard from Sophia, and that was making me more than a little anxious.

"Why don't you come back to bed for a while," Deliah suggested.

"I have to go to work. The captain asked to meet with me and Petty about something."

"Okay, well I've got two new girls coming over later. Do you think that you could join me?" she asked seductively.

It was on the tip of my tongue to say no, but doing that would raise red flags with Deliah. Initially telling her about Sophia had brought out some jealousy in her that I'd never seen, but she'd managed to keep her cuckoo in the clock. I'd be stupid to bring out her insecurities again.

"I'm with that," I replied, turning around so I could pull her into my arms and kiss her softly on the lips. I'd meant this kiss to be sweet, but she made it clear that she had other intentions. Given the fact that we were both already naked only made it easier for her to grab my dick and breathe life into it with her skilled touch.

"Babe, I gotta work," I whispered against her lips.

"You better make it quick then," she replied before biting my lip hard.

I picked her up by her juicy ass cheeks and spun her around until I had her back pressed up against the picture window. If anyone happened to be walking past her bedroom window, they were about to get more than an eye full of action. I pushed my dick deep inside her, hard enough to snatch her breath away, but before I could pull back and deliver a follow up blow, there was a knock on the door.

"I-ignore it," Deliah demanded, kissing me frantically.

I was happy to oblige now that I was submerged in her underwater cavern, and I immediately pulled out and dove back inside her with the same intensity. I only managed two strokes though before the knocking came again.

"G-go away!" Deliah yelled impatiently.

"Detective Pettybone is here," Cassandra replied.

"Then go fuck him or s-suck his dick. Just go away!" Deliah insisted.

"Max, we gotta go," Petty hollered from right outside the bedroom door.

Hearing his voice stopped my movements completely, and I could tell by the look of frustration on Deliah's face that she knew it was over for now.

"I'll meet you out front in a minute," I replied.

I could tell that Deliah was expecting me to put her down, but instead, I carried her to the bed, laid her on her back, and started pounding her pussy like a man possessed.

"M-max, w-w-wait," she stammered, trying to lock her legs around my waist.

I grabbed her right leg and put it on my left shoulder, changing the angle of my onslaught and leaving her unable to do anything except moan. With the speed and force of my strokes, I was able to make both of us cum within a few minutes, and while she was lying in bed trying to stop her legs from shaking uncontrollably, I was getting dressed.

"I'll be back when I can," I said, dropping a quick kiss on her lips before heading for the door.

I pulled it open to find Cassandra standing on the other side, smiling.

"Finish her off," I said, winking as I moved past her.

I found Petty waiting for me on the front porch, and one look at him told me that something was wrong.

"You're early. What's up?" I asked, pulling my T-shirt on.

"Captain wants to see us now. We just caught a fresh homicide."

"Homicide? That ain't our playground," I replied, surprised.

"I'll explain on the way," he said, leading the way down the steps to his car.

I climbed in the passenger seat and we quickly got on the move.

"Talk to me," I said.

"Sometime after three a.m., a man was gunned down on the strip, shot seven times at point blank range with a Berretta 9mm. Apparently, the victim and the shooter were lifelong friends, but a disagreement turned real ugly real quick."

"Okay, well so far it sounds like a standard case for homicide," I replied, confused.

"Both of them were high out of their minds. Do you want to guess what they were high on?" Petty asked, looking over at me.

It took all of my strength and willpower not to let a scream full of rage loose, but I managed to clench my jaw hard enough to make it ache. This was part of what I'd been worried about in the last few weeks because Saint's dope invading Vegas had the potential to affect people I cared about. I couldn't allow that to keep happening.

"I understand why the captain wants to see us, because nobody wanted that dope anywhere near here. What I don't understand is why we're working the homicide angle," I said.

"We're not exactly working the case. We're just getting all the facts of it to see if we can trace the heroin to anyone in Vegas. The captain wants us to hit the ground running, and apparently, she's got us meeting with some important people because she wants us in her office *now*."

"It's gonna be a long day," I mumbled, pulling my phone out so I could text Deliah the good news.

Once I did that, I was tempted to text Sophia, but I knew the smart play was to wait a little while longer. No matter how hard that was to do. Within fifteen minutes, Petty had us at the police station, but when we got to our captain's office, we saw something that had us looking at each other.

"Suits means one thing," I whispered.

"Feds," Petty replied softly.

I didn't know what was going on, but I knew that shit was definitely about to get interesting.

"Appreciate you two making it in on such short notice," Captain Valencia said, waving us both into the room.

Simone Valencia was a half-white, half-Puerto Rican beauty, but if you thought her looks were all she had to offer, then you had her fucked up. She was one of two supervisors over the narcotics division, and she'd never spent a second on her back to get to her position. She worked her ass off, and she expected everyone around her to do the same.

"No problem, Capt, what do you need?" I asked.

Once her office door closed she nodded towards the two clean-cut, middle-aged white men in the matching black suits seated on the loveseat against the wall.

"I'm Agent Myers and this is Agent Roysdan. We're DEA. We're here to speak with you about Fabian Santoro."

Petty and I exchanged a quick look that conveyed the same message. Oh shit.

"What about Saint?" I asked.

"We're aware of the help that you two provided recently in Fresno with regards to identifying the location of a major stash house, and that you did this very quietly. We'd like you're help delivering a more permanent blow to Saint and his organization," Agent Myers said.

For a few seconds I didn't say anything. I simply looked from one agent to another, trying to feel out their bullshit.

"I'll bite. What type of help were you looking for us to provide?" I asked.

"Not both of you; just you, Detective Cooper." Agent Roysdan stated.

I looked at Petty again, expecting him to be just about ready to cuss these Feds out, but the expression on his face was one of curiosity and calm.

"We're a team, so - "

"That may be true, but only one of you can perform the necessary task, and that's *you*, Detective Cooper. Or should I call you Mad Max?" Agent Myers asked.

It was clear that these Feds were out to get my attention, but it was obvious to me that they might not understand how bad of an idea that was.

"Cut the bullshit, and say what you gotta say," I replied.

"Cooper," Captain Valencia said in warning.

"It's okay, Simone, we need him to be exactly who he is," Agent Roysdan said.

"It's come to our attention that your path has crossed with Mrs. Santoro when she was much younger and much more innocent. For that reason, we believe that you're the one person who can do what everyone else has failed to do, and that's flip Sophia Santoro," Agent Myers stated.

"Flip her how? She's married to Saint, so she can't testify against him," I replied.

"Detective Cooper, we're the United States government. There's a way around everything, just like there's a way to use the valuable information Mrs. Santoro had in that pretty little head of hers that doesn't involve a courtroom," Agent Roysdan said.

"So you think a motherfucker like Saint is just gonna let his wife be buddy-buddy with a cop because her and I go way back? Not hardly," I replied sarcastically.

"Sophia isn't your way in. Saint is," Agent Myers said.

"Huh?" I asked, completely confused.

"Right now, Saint has found himself detained out in L.A. without any explanation, and he's been given no access to a phone to call his lawyer. Recently we became aware that Saint had a mole inside the DEA who has been feeding him information for years, but that agent met with an untimely demise. We want you to take his place. We want you to fly to L.A. and get Saint out, which will demonstrate your value to him," Agent Myers said.

"How do you think that's gonna work? I don't know - "

"Everything that you need to know about the agent who was working for Saint is in this file," Agent Roysdan said, passing me a thick manila envelope.

I was still trying to wrap my mind around what Agent Myers had said, but I took the folder and opened it to give myself time to process. I could immediately tell that they weren't lying when they said this file contained everything, because the first thing I saw was a kindergarten progress report. The dead agent's name was Boyd Lewis, and I now had his life's story in my hand.

"So you want me to act like I knew Boyd Lewis?" I asked.

"No, we want you to become his best friend and silent partner. You knowing details about Boyd and his business with Saint, plus you showing up to save Saint, should let his guard down enough for him to be curious about you. From there he'll test you, but he'll never trust you. Once you're in, you've gotta convince Sophia to flip," Agent Myers replied.

"What makes you certain that she'll trust me" I mean, it's been a long time since we've communicated," I said.

"Has it?" Agent Myers asked.

It took everything in me not to look over at Petty because I knew he heard the sarcasm in the agent's tone, and that could mean bad things for us. Agent Myers took his time reaching in his pocket, but all he came out with was his cell phone. I didn't know what he was up to, but I was getting a bad feeling. Once he turned the phone's screen in my direction, I knew my feelings of impending doom were justified.

"I gotta admit, I do see the resemblance between you and little Angelo, but only because I'm looking for it. And I can tell by your lack of surprise that I'm not telling you anything that you don't know," Agent Myers said, smiling slightly.

"So let's say that I agree. How deep will my cover be?" I asked.

"You'll be an official employee of the United States drug enforcement agency before you walk out of this room, with all the credentials that Boyd Lewis had. If you're checked out, no matter how thoroughly, you'll be exactly who you say you are. All you have to do is convince Saint of your willingness to bend, break, and bypass the law," Captain Valencia said.

"What happens to Sophia and Angelo when this is all over?" I asked.

"That's up to you and Sophia, but the government will give you carte blanche when it comes to relocating all of you. *If* you accomplish the objective of bringing down Saint," Agent Roysdan replied.

I knew that what was being asked of me wasn't anything small, and it most definitely could cost me my life. If my only son wasn't worth my life though, then who was? I finally looked at Petty to gauge what he was feeling about all this, and even though I saw his apprehension, I knew he'd back my play.

"If I do this, then Detective Pettybone does it with me. You get him the same DEA credentials as me, and let me worry about what role he plays," I said.

"That's not gonna - "

"It's non-negotiable, Agent Roysdan, and don't waste my time like you're the only one negotiating from a position of power. If you could've gotten to Sophia by now, you would've. I can, so what do you wanna do?" I asked.

This time it was Roysdan and Myers who exchanged a long look, but everyone in the room knew what was gonna happen.

"Agreed. Just try not to get everyone you love killed."

Chapter 20
Twenty-nine hours later

"Mr. Santoro, I'm - "

"I don't give a fuck *who* you are, I'm not saying shit without my lawyer. It don't matter how long you motherfuckers hold me, I'm still not saying shit without my lawyer," he stated angrily.

"Saint, do me a favor and shut the fuck up," I said, shutting the door to the interrogation room and taking a seat across from him at the metal table he was handcuffed to.

The anger in his eyes was easy to see, and I was betting that it was due to the fact that nobody talked to him like that. His anger didn't move me though because I knew that the only thing a lion respected was a bigger, fiercer lion. I reached into the inside pocket of my suit jacket and pulled out my newly-printed DEA credentials.

"My name is Agent Cooper, and it's in your best interest to listen to what I'm about to say because it's the difference between the good life and no life at all. In a few minutes there's gonna be a knock on the door behind me, and someone will enter to inform us that you've been released into my custody. After that, I'm gonna handcuff you and take you to a more secure location where we can talk about - "

"I don't have anything to say, so - "

"Saint, don't interrupt me again," I warned in a deadly whisper.

There was an intense stare down between us for several seconds, but he blinked first. Before I could open my mouth to speak, there was a knock on the door and it was opened.

"Agent Cooper, the paperwork is done and you're free to take him," a young male police officer said.

The door was quickly closed after this announcement was made, leaving Saint and me alone again. I put my badge back in my pocket and removed a handcuff key from my pants pocket. After reaching across the table and uncuffing him, I pulled out my own cuffs and moved around the table towards him.

"Hands behind your back," I demanded.

"I don't know what this is about, but you obviously don't know who you're dealing with."

"I know *exactly* who I'm dealing with, Saint. You're just confusing me with those who are scared of you," I replied, putting the cuffs on him and locking them tight enough to cut off his circulation.

Seeing him flinch made me smile, especially since I knew that I'd have to play nice shortly.

"Smart people *are* scared of me. I've got a *long* reach," he said arrogantly.

My response was to shove him roughly towards the door, hoping he'd somehow end up on his face. As expected, we made it out of the police station without any problems or delays, but I knew that that would be easy compared to what was next to come. I quickly pushed Saint into the back of my borrowed black Chevy Suburban, hopped in the driver's seat, and got us on the move. While I was driving, I went over in my mind what was about to take place, knowing that it had to be perfect in order to have the desired effect. Surprisingly, Saint remained calm and quiet for the first hour of our drive, but somehow I knew that wouldn't last.

"Yo, where the fuck are you taking me?" he asked.

"Home."

"Bullshit, I don't live nowhere near here. Where are you taking me?" he asked again.

"Do I detect fear in your voice?" I asked, laughing softly.

I knew it wasn't smart to antagonize him when I was so close to showing my hand, but I *really* don't like this mother-fucker.

"I fear nothing and no one. Ask about me," he replied aggressively.

"I know all about you, Saint. In fact, I know more than you think I know."

"I doubt that. You law enforcement types always think you know more than you do," he replied.

"I know where we're going," I said sarcastically.

He didn't have shit to say about that, but I didn't mind because the sound of his voice was annoying as fuck. We reached our destination a short fifteen minutes later.

"I don't live in no fucking warehouse," Saint said, obviously frustrated.

"No, but you do handle business in warehouses. So let's handle a little business, and then I'll take you home," I replied, opening my door and getting out.

Once I got him out, I led him to the side door of the abandoned warehouse and we stepped into the scene that would change everything. Twenty feet from the door sat a man strapped to a chair with a gag in his mouth. I didn't have to ask Saint if he knew the man because the hesitation in his steps said it all.

"W-what the fuck is this?" Saint asked.

"I believe this is one of your top lieutenants, Mario Rodriguez."

"I know who he is, but what the fuck is he doing being held hostage? Do you not know who you're fucking with?" Saint asked, looking at me with eyes flaming with hate and anger.

"I know *exactly* who I'm fucking with, and like I told you earlier, I know more than you think. Ain't that right, Mario?"

I asked, walking over to the now-squirming man and pulling the gag from his mouth.

"Please, *please*, Saint! I didn't have a choice, I swear to God that I had no goddamn choice!" Mario insisted desperately.

"Mario, what the fuck are you talking about?" Saint asked, confused.

"Oh, allow me to enlighten you. What Mario is rambling about is the deal he tried to make to sell you out in order to save his son that got caught with a kilo of your heroin," I replied sweetly.

"No way would he betray me," Saint said, looking at me.

The look in his eyes was less than confident, but I knew how to remove all traces of doubt. From my inside jacket pocket I pulled a piece of paper, which I unfolded as I walked back to Saint so I could hold it up in front of his face. What he was reading was a form to start the procedure for Mario Rodriguez to become a federal witness in the RICO case against Fabian Santoro. And it was signed by Mario himself. I couldn't deny the enjoyment I felt at watching the blood drain from Saint's face, even though I knew it was only momentary. Suddenly, Saint erupted with fluent Spanish leveled at Mario. I couldn't quite follow what he was saying, but the meaning was clear. He wanted to kill Mario.

"Calm down, calm down, it's okay," I said.

"How the fuck is this okay?"

"It's okay because I'm a friend of Boyd's," I replied.

That statement changed Saint's whole demeanor, causing him to go from pissed to slightly hopeful.

"Boyd sent you? Why didn't he just come himself?" Saint asked skeptically.

"Because Boyd's dead. When and how he died are not important, but what is important is that you paid him handsomely enough to have an insurance plan. I'm that insurance plan," I replied.

"Boyd never told me about you," Saint said.

"And why would he? Some people play chess by moving pieces, while other people play by seeing the board in at least three dimensions. Boyd could see the board, and he knew that a man of your means needed more than plans A through Z, you needed your own alphabet. I can understand why you might not believe me though, but ask yourself this: if I was lying, why would we be here right now," I replied, looking around.

The contemplation was evident on Saint's face, and I knew that I was only one move away from checkmate.

"If that's the case, then why do I still have handcuffs on?" Saint asked.

"I can get those off of you right now," I said, pulling my Glock .27 from my shoulder holster and chambering a round.

I turned swiftly back around to face Mario, raised the gun, and fired off five shots in rapid succession. Four bullets tore through his chest, and the final one pushed his nose through the back of his head. I holstered my gun, uncuffed Saint, and started walking towards the exit.

"You coming?" I asked once I got to the door and saw that he was still standing in front of the late Mario Rodriguez.

He was slow to move, and when he locked eyes with me, I saw complete confusion swimming in the deep waters of his soul. I led the way to the SUV and once Saint climbed in I pointed us in the direction of his home. I had no doubts that he was used to using long silences to make people extremely uncomfortable, but this tactic wouldn't work on me. I knew beneath his confusion he was impressed and grateful, but I doubted that he'd express either of those things to me. He was the boss, and he would need to reassert his authority to feel comfortable moving forward.

"What field office are you based out of?" Saints asked, fifteen minutes into our drive.

"I'm primarily in Vegas, but I'm thinking about transferring to D.C soon."

"That's not gonna happen, I want you on the West Coast so you can keep a close eye on things because if the governments is trying to build a RICO case, then that means they want me bad," he replied.

"I can't stop my life just because - "

"You can and you *will*. You don't need to worry about promotions or 401k plans because you work for me now, and you'll be taken care of," Saint said.

I waited just the right amount of time before speaking again. "I appreciate the opportunity," I replied humbly.

"Yeah, well, don't think taking care of that situation back there earns you brownie points. I've got plenty of shooters, and what I need are your connections within the DEA, and any other agency coming after me."

"Understood," I replied.

With the business made clear, we rode on in silence, each of us trapped in our own thoughts. As crazy as the past few hours had been, including committing cold-blooded murder, I know this was the easy part. Despite Sophia's feelings for me, I knew that it would be like pulling teeth to convince her to betray her husband. It was too late for me to go back now though.

"We need to make a stop before you take me home. I want you to go to this address," he said, tapping keys on the tracks GPS.

A development of office buildings came up, which made me breathe a sigh of relief because I thought he was about to lead me down some back alley. It took me forty minutes to get him where he wanted to go, but he was in and out within five minutes.

"Here," he said, tossing a brand new cell phone into my lap.

"Thanks, but - "

"No buts. That's the only phone that you and I will ever talk on. It's encrypted, and you better not give anybody the number or we're gonna have problems," he said, opening the packaging on his own new phone.

"I got you."

"Good, now take me home," he demanded.

The way he was talking to me made me wanna beat the skin off of his face, but instead, I put the truck in gear and got back on the road. A half an hour later I was pulling into the circular driveway of his eight bedroom L.A. mansion.

"There's two things I need from you, and they're non-negotiable," he said once I'd brought us to a stop.

"I'm listening."

"I need that piece of paper you showed me, and I need your gun," he replied seriously.

My first reaction was to say, "Bitch, what?" But I bit my tongue while reaching in my pocket. I knew he wanted the paperwork so he could verify it, and he wanted the gun because it was dirty with the added bonus of being made that way by a dirty DEA agent. After passing him the paperwork I handed him my pistol with the handle facing him. I wasn't the least bit surprised when he put the gun to my forehead.

"Give me one good reason not to pull the trigger and then make your body disappear," he said.

"Because that would only add to your problems, not make them disappear," I replied calmly.

The seconds that ticked by were long, but I didn't flinch nor did I show fear because either reaction would guarantee death. Saint needed to know that I had ice water in my veins.

"Come with me," he said, lowering the gun after a long minute, stepping out of the truck.

I took a much-needed deep breath and followed his lead, making sure to feel my backup gun tucked into the back of my slacks. I followed him up the walkway and through the front door. The commotion was instantaneous.

"Thank God!" Sophia exclaimed, rushing into Saint's arms, where she was scooped up and kissed thoroughly.

Observing this had my hand itching to reach for my gun and splatter his brains all over the smooth marble floors, but I resisted.

"Babe, where the fuck have you been? I've been worried...sick," Sophia said her voice trailing off as our eyes locked and sheer terror gripped her.

"It's a long story, but I'm good thanks to my new associate. This is Agent Cooper and he's DEA," Saint replied, turning towards me to make a proper introduction.

If he'd been looking at his wife he'd have known instantly that something was wrong, but thankfully, she shook that shit off.

"I don't understand. How did the DEA help you? *Why* would they?" she asked slowly.

"It's a long story, but I'll explain everything. I don't keep anything from my wife, Cooper, so you and I are gonna sit down and bring her up to speed," Saint said.

"Fine by me," I readily agreed.

"But babe - "

"No buts. I don't need you stressing, so I'm gonna tell you what's going on. Then you and our baby can go relax," Saint said, patting on Sophia's stomach.

"B-baby?" I choked out somehow.

"Yeah, my queen is pregnant, only a few weeks though. Still, she's got a very important life growing inside her, and I'll do whatever I have to in order to protect our child. *Whatever.*"

To Be Continued...
Sins of a Hustla 2
Coming Soon

Submission Guideline

Submit the first three chapters of your completed manuscript to ldpsubmissions@gmail.com, subject line: Your book's title. The manuscript must be in a .doc file and sent as an attachment. Document should be in Times New Roman, double spaced and in size 12 font. Also, provide your synopsis and full contact information. If sending multiple submissions, they must each be in a separate email.

Have a story but no way to send it electronically? You can still submit to LDP/Ca$h Presents. Send in the first three chapters, written or typed, of your completed manuscript to:

LDP: Submissions Dept
Po Box 870494
Mesquite, Tx 75187

DO NOT send original manuscript. Must be a duplicate.

Provide your synopsis and a cover letter containing your full contact information.

Thanks for considering LDP and Ca$h Presents.

Coming Soon from Lock Down Publications/Ca$h Presents

BOW DOWN TO MY GANGSTA

By **Ca$h**

TORN BETWEEN TWO

By **Coffee**

BLOOD STAINS OF A SHOTTA **III**

By **Jamaica**

STEADY MOBBIN **III**

By **Marcellus Allen**

BLOOD OF A BOSS **V**

By **Askari**

LOYAL TO THE GAME **IV**

LIFE OF SIN

By **T.J. & Jelissa**

A DOPEBOY'S PRAYER **II**

By **Eddie "Wolf" Lee**

IF LOVING YOU IS WRONG… **III**

LOVE ME EVEN WHEN IT HURTS **II**

By **Jelissa**

TRUE SAVAGE **VI**

By **Chris Green**

BLAST FOR ME **III**

A BRONX TALE

By **Ghost**

ADDICTIED TO THE DRAMA **III**

By **Jamila Mathis**

LIPSTICK KILLAH **III**

CRIME OF PASSION **II**

By **Mimi**

WHAT BAD BITCHES DO **III**

KILL ZONE **II**

By **Aryanna**

THE COST OF LOYALTY **II**

By **Kweli**

SHE FELL IN LOVE WITH A REAL ONE **II**

By **Tamara Butler**

LOVE SHOULDN'T HURT **III**

RENEGADE BOYS **II**

By **Meesha**

CORRUPTED BY A GANGSTA **IV**

By **Destiny Skai**

A GANGSTER'S CODE **III**

By **J-Blunt**

KING OF NEW YORK III

By **T.J. Edwards**

CUM FOR ME **IV**

By **Ca$h & Company**

GORILLAS IN THE BAY

De'Kari

THE STREETS ARE CALLING

Duquie Wilson

KINGPIN KILLAZ II

Hood Rich

STEADY MOBBIN' **III**

Marcellus Allen

SINS OF A HUSTLA II

ASAD

HER MAN, MINE'S TOO **II**

Nicole Goosby

GORILLAZ IN THE BAY **II**

DE'KARI

TRIGGADALE II

Elijah R. Freeman

THE STREETS ARE CALLING **II**

Duquie Wilson

Available Now

RESTRAINING ORDER **I & II**

By **CA$H & Coffee**

LOVE KNOWS NO BOUNDARIES **I II & III**

By **Coffee**

RAISED AS A GOON I, II, III & IV

BRED BY THE SLUMS I, II, III

BLAST FOR ME I & II

ROTTEN TO THE CORE I III

By **Ghost**

LAY IT DOWN **I & II**

LAST OF A DYING BREED

BLOOD STAINS OF A SHOTTA I & II

By **Jamaica**

LOYAL TO THE GAME

LOYAL TO THE GAME II

LOYAL TO THE GAME III

By **TJ & Jelissa**

BLOODY COMMAS I & II

SKI MASK CARTEL I II & III

KING OF NEW YORK I II

By **T.J. Edwards**

IF LOVING HIM IS WRONG…I & II

LOVE ME EVEN WHEN IT HURTS

By **Jelissa**

WHEN THE STREETS CLAP BACK I & II III

By **Jibril Williams**

A DISTINGUISHED THUG STOLE MY HEART I II & III

LOVE SHOULDN'T HURT I II

RENEGADE BOYS

By **Meesha**

A GANGSTER'S CODE I & II

By **J-Blunt**

PUSH IT TO THE LIMIT

By **Bre' Hayes**

BLOOD OF A BOSS **I, II, III & IV**

By **Askari**

THE STREETS BLEED MURDER **I, II & III**

THE HEART OF A GANGSTA I II& III

By **Jerry Jackson**

CUM FOR ME

CUM FOR ME 2

CUM FOR ME 3

An **LDP Erotica Collaboration**

BRIDE OF A HUSTLA **I II & II**

THE FETTI GIRLS **I, II& III**

CORRUPTED BY A GANGSTA I, II & III

By **Destiny Skai**

WHEN A GOOD GIRL GOES BAD

By **Adrienne**

A GANGSTER'S REVENGE **I II III & IV**

THE BOSS MAN'S DAUGHTERS

THE BOSS MAN'S DAUGHTERS II

THE BOSSMAN'S DAUGHTERS III

THE BOSSMAN'S DAUGHTERS IV

THE BOSS MAN'S DAUGHTERS **V**

A SAVAGE LOVE **I & II**

BAE BELONGS TO ME

A HUSTLER'S DECEIT I, II

WHAT BAD BITCHES DO I, II

By **Aryanna**

A KINGPIN'S AMBITON

A KINGPIN'S AMBITION **II**

I MURDER FOR THE DOUGH

By **Ambitious**

TRUE SAVAGE

TRUE SAVAGE II

TRUE SAVAGE **III**

TRUE SAVAGE **IV**

TRUE SAVAGE **V**

By **Chris Green**

A DOPEBOY'S PRAYER

By **Eddie "Wolf" Lee**

THE KING CARTEL **I, II & III**

By **Frank Gresham**

THESE NIGGAS AIN'T LOYAL **I, II & III**

By **Nikki Tee**

GANGSTA SHYT **I II &III**

By **CATO**

THE ULTIMATE BETRAYAL

By **Phoenix**

BOSS'N UP **I , II & III**

By **Royal Nicole**

I LOVE YOU TO DEATH

By Destiny J

I RIDE FOR MY HITTA

I STILL RIDE FOR MY HITTA

By **Misty Holt**

LOVE & CHASIN' PAPER

By **Qay Crockett**

TO DIE IN VAIN

By **ASAD**

BROOKLYN HUSTLAZ

By **Boogsy Morina**

BROOKLYN ON LOCK I & II

By **Sonovia**

GANGSTA CITY

By **Teddy Duke**

A DRUG KING AND HIS DIAMOND I & II III

A DOPEMAN'S RICHES

HER MAN, MINE'S TOO

By **Nicole Goosby**

TRAPHOUSE KING **I II & III**

KINGPIN KILLAZ

By **Hood Rich**

LIPSTICK KILLAH **I, II**

CRIME OF PASSION

By **Mimi**

STEADY MOBBN' **I, II**

By **Marcellus Allen**

WHO SHOT YA **I, II**

Renta

GORILLAZ IN THE BAY

DE'KARI

TRIGGADALE

Elijah R. Freeman

GOD BLESS THE TRAPPERS I, II, III

THESE SCANDALOUS STREETS I, II, III

FEAR MY GANGSTA I, II

THESE STREETS DON'T LOVE NOBODY I, II

Tranay Adams

ASAD

THE STREETS ARE CALLING
Duquie Wilson
SINS OF A HUSTLA
ASAD

BOOKS BY LDP'S CEO, CA$H

TRUST IN NO MAN

TRUST IN NO MAN 2

TRUST IN NO MAN 3

BONDED BY BLOOD

SHORTY GOT A THUG

THUGS CRY

THUGS CRY 2

THUGS CRY 3

TRUST NO BITCH

TRUST NO BITCH 2

TRUST NO BITCH 3

TIL MY CASKET DROPS

RESTRAINING ORDER

RESTRAINING ORDER 2

IN LOVE WITH A CONVICT

Coming Soon

BONDED BY BLOOD 2

BOW DOWN TO MY GANGSTA

ASAD